BONNIE
&
CLYDE

*Also by Bill Brooks
in Large Print:*

Buscadero
The Stone Garden

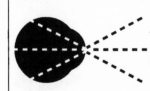

This Large Print Book carries the
Seal of Approval of N.A.V.H.

BONNIE

CLYDE

A Love Story

BILL BROOKS

JESSAMINE COUNTY PUBLIC LIBRARY
600 South Main Street
Nicholasville, KY 40356
(859) 885-3523

Thorndike Press • Waterville, Maine

LT
BROO

3 2530 60573 0751

Copyright © 2004 by Bill Brooks

All rights reserved.

This is a work of fiction. All the characters and events portrayed in this novel are either fictitious or are used fictitiously.

Published in 2004 by arrangement with Tom Doherty Associates, LLC.

Thorndike Press® Large Print Americana.

The tree indicium is a trademark of Thorndike Press.

The text of this Large Print edition is unabridged. Other aspects of the book may vary from the original edition.

Set in 16 pt. Plantin.

Printed in the United States on permanent paper.

Library of Congress Cataloging-in-Publication Data

Brooks, Bill, 1943–
    Bonnie and Clyde : a love story / Bill Brooks.
        p. cm.
    ISBN 0-7862-6324-5 (lg. print : hc : alk. paper)
    1. Barrow, Clyde, 1909–1934 — Fiction.   2. Parker,
Bonnie, 1910–1934 — Fiction.   3. Criminals — Fiction.
    4. Large type books.   I. Title.
    PS3552.R65863B66 2004b
        813′.54—dc22   2003071176

For Jeff Rackham, writer, friend

National Association for Visually Handicapped
---------------------- *serving the partially seeing*

As the Founder/CEO of NAVH, the only national health agency solely devoted to those who, although not totally blind, have an eye disease which could lead to serious visual impairment, I am pleased to recognize Thorndike Press* as one of the leading publishers in the large print field.

Founded in 1954 in San Francisco to prepare large print textbooks for partially seeing children, NAVH became the pioneer and standard setting agency in the preparation of large type.

Today, those publishers who meet our standards carry the prestigious "Seal of Approval" indicating high quality large print. We are delighted that Thorndike Press is one of the publishers whose titles meet these standards. We are also pleased to recognize the significant contribution Thorndike Press is making in this important and growing field.

Lorraine H. Marchi, L.H.D.
Founder/CEO
NAVH

* Thorndike Press encompasses the following imprints: Thorndike, Wheeler, Walker and Large Print Press.

Texas heat wobbles like liquid glass off the hardpan. An old man with a dying cow stands in his field and watches a tan Ford kicking up a tunnel of dust on the road to Dallas.

Sumbitch is moving out, the old man thinks, scratching a scab under his hat. Time the dust settles again, his cow has died. The cow's passing seems to fall right in line with most things been happening lately. The land and all it holds is run near to ruin. Banks closing by the dozens. This on the heels of three hard years of drought. Hoover's in the White House staying mum. Brother, can you spare a dime. They say men are jumping out of windows in Dallas and Chicago and New York City, too. Wouldn't be surprised. I'd jump out a damn window too if I had one to jump out of.

The old man hears the drone of the V-8

like an angry yellow jacket until it is faded into the heat, swallowed up by the buzz of cicadas. Grasshoppers came through the past spring chewing grass and crops to stubble — that which would grow in the first place.

Leans, tries to spit. Mouth so dry, he can't. Like everything else — mouth's full of dust and no hope.

Then the old man remembers where he's seen that particular Ford with those big whitewall tires.

Was it carrying two people? Three? Went by so fast it was hard to tell.

He stands there watching into the long nothingness at the end of the road. Dallas: forty-three long miles. A world away if you've got no cause to go there.

Yes sir, I do believe I have seen that V-8 before.

He walks to the house where the old woman is running a hot iron over a faded housedress she intends to wear to church that morning — its red faded to pink, its print of flowers like a distant wilted garden.

"You need to go clean up, Henry."

Even the Lord Jesus Christ couldn't save any of them. He knows it, suspects she does too. But women have fortitude beyond that of a man, have an innate sense of trust in spiritual things. She's had it all her life. It is that, he believes, that has caused her to stick to him through six kids, a dozen jobs, untold moves.

"I guess I just seen something," he says.

Her mouth is grim over the task of trying to iron the wrinkles out of the freshly washed and line-dried dress that has the smell of summer in it still.

"What'd you see, old man?"

He paces the floor there in the kitchen where she's ironing. The floor slopes slightly down toward the creek like it's thirsty and been trying to get down there ever since the first nail was driven home.

"I guess I by God seen Clyde Barrow run past here just now."

"Clyde Barrow?" She stops the iron and holds it inches above the fabric of the best piece of clothing she owns. It wouldn't pay to scorch it.

"I recognized his automobile."

"Where do you think he was headed?"

"Only one place he could along that there road. Dallas."

"Wonder the police aren't on his heels."

"I'd reckon they will be if they ain't already."

"Did you see Bonnie with him?"

"I think I did, and maybe one or two others in the car."

"Oh, Lord, you think they . . . ?"

"What else would they be doing running fast like that?"

A moment's pause is all she'll allow, then sets to finishing the ironing of her dress.

"You best get cleaned up."

He washes his hands at the sink, pumping hard the handle, once, twice, three times. The water is clear and cold and has the taste of iron to it when he turns his hands into cups to drink.

"I hope they took down a bank," he says. "I surely do. Those damn bankers is nothing but thieves themselves."

"Henry, that's no way to talk on the Sabbath."

"What happened to us, Lil?"

"Whatever do you mean?"

"I mean, what happened to us to have wound up like we have? Just some old folks trying to make a living out of nothing. You having to wear faded old dresses and me in overalls and clods on my feet. It ain't the way I ever imagined I'd turn out when I was young."

"You're talking like a fool, Henry. You turned out a good man. And me, a good woman."

"I know you turned out good, Lil. But we let life throw a loop around us — not like them." He thumbs toward the road that is quiet again under the brown waves of heat.

"Don't regret we didn't turn out to be criminals, Henry. That's a fool's way of thinking."

"Oh, I ain't never wanted to break the law. But I sure never wanted to end up like this, neither."

She sets the iron on its heel and drops the dress down over her head and fits herself into it, smoothing the flare of her skirt as she does. Pats at the pin curls in her hair, casts him a sidelong look. Fixes her hat on her head, the little net down over her eyes. Through it she can see the worn tired face of her husband. Can see restless eyes and behind them restless thoughts.

"It don't pay to regret things, Henry."

"I know it don't."

She takes his hand and pats it.

"Get your good hat on," she says.

He follows her out to the flivver, a skin of dust covers its black coat. She takes her hankie and wipes the seat before sitting while he settles in behind the wheel.

"Well, you going to start the car?" she

11

says after several seconds; he's just been sitting there staring through the grimy windshield — staring off in the direction of Dallas so far away he can only imagine it from the time he was there a year ago.

Off in the distance they can hear the church bell gonging — a heavy sound like sorrow.

"We'll go get on our knees and pray, Henry."

But all he can set his mind on is how much more fascinating life would be if he were driving a fast Ford with a beautiful girl like Bonnie Parker sitting beside him and a valise full of bank money.

"Maybe it wasn't them at all," Lil says.

"Maybe not," he says and starts the flivver and rides over the ruts toward the sound of the church bell.

1

Love Like Steel

Hear the cries of lonely men. Hear their desperate mourn. Jail doors shut hard like jaws snapping closed, like the gnashing of metal teeth. Snorts and sniffs; the young and weak are prey. Hard eyes watch, their feral lips drawn back in devils' grins as young, lean torsos bend with fear.

"Come close here, boy, let me have a look at you."

Clyde prays all night that one of them won't settle a leering gaze on him. Prays hard, *Oh, Jesus, don't let one of them take notice, take and pin me down, take and turn me queer.*

He's smallish, slender as a boy, barely five feet seven, a hundred and twenty pounds. No match for the hardened cons with hardened muscles and hardened brains. But give him a gun, a pistol, and you'll see how things even out. But in the joint, no guns allowed. Knives maybe, if

13

you can make your own and hide it from the screws. Knives and fists are all a guy has got to defend himself with from the craven lifers, those men who have long forgot the soft feel of a woman — who no longer care.

"Come here, boy, let me have a closer look at you."

The hot shower's sting of water against bare skin there on display for others to barter over is no relief at all.

Their eyes watch and watch. You're like a dame in those eyes. The lights turned out, what does it matter?

"Come here, boy."

His nerves are a wreck. Every time somebody coughs. Every time he hears footsteps coming down the tier. Every time he hears the groan of weaker men like himself in the night, the slap of a hand against flesh, something goes loose in his bowels. He's seen in passing, guys with knives to their throats, their eyes bugged wide as they are escorted into some recess out of sight of screws. Taunting, teasing, the blade against the jugular takes all the nerve out of you. Some guys learn to like it, he never would.

"Don't move or I'll cut you."

Knowing any second it could be him.

Knowing that sooner or later it *will* be him.

One guy, a young guy named Danny with dark Cajun eyes fresh in from the streets, lasts not even two weeks.

Taken by a big spade everyone calls Chicago Willy.

"Come here, white boy, let me have a look at you."

"No sir. I ain't here to find no trouble."

"I know you ain't. But you see, in a place like this, a pretty little white boy like you needs some *pertection*."

"No sir, I can take care of myself, thank you very much, sir."

But that night, Clyde hears things. Hears a scuffling sound over in Chicago Willy's cell. Hears a sound like what you might hear when a dog takes a cat — a something "quick" and terrible sound.

"Oh!" He thinks it's the Cajun's shrill voice that says it. Then some scuffling going on, then little cries, like a child being whipped.

Can't be, Clyde tells himself. How is it Chicago Willy can get his hands on the boy? Ain't the guards watching things? But the hard cons know Chicago Willy's got even the guards afraid of him. He tells them he'll keep order in the block as long as they don't fool with him, he'll make

15

their job easy and run things smooth. But sometimes they got to look the other way. Sometimes they got to turn they heads. 'Cause a man has got certain needs, you know? Sure, we know, Willy. Just keep the order; just make our jobs easy.

Scuffling. Sound of fist striking bone. More whimpers.

"Shut up now. Go along with it. Shut up now."

Sounds of a beating down. Every con who has been inside knows the scenario.

Clyde grits his teeth.

Next day the boy is found with his throat cut in the shower — his blood running like red ink down the drain. His small penis shriveled in death. He is as pale as milk. He is crumpled as though having been hit by a car. And whatever his eyes saw in that moment before death, they are never going to reveal.

Clyde writes his mother, pleads with her to get his sentence commuted.

Tell the governor I'm only twenty-one. While he's waiting for a reply, he pays a con to chop off two of his toes so he can get sent to the hospital — someplace a guy like Chicago Willy can't get to him so easily.

Surprisingly, the bite of the ax is hardly

more than a burn that dissolves to painlessness. But, Jesus, later his foot throbs like a machine, sends wires of pain up his leg, into his groin, all the way to his brain. Throbs and throbs.

The medico smiles and says, "Better chopped toes than taking it up the ass, eh?"

It's thirteen more years if his mother can't get the governor to commute his sentence. He's only got eight toes left.

A letter arrives from Bonnie.

Dearest Darling, I don't think I can stand not seeing you for thirteen years. We'll both be pretty old! Sugar, what are we going to do? She writes how much she misses him and how she lays in bed every night and pretends her pillow is him and how she holds him close to her naked body and rubs herself against it.

Promise me when you get out you won't do any more jobs, sugar. Oh, and I lost my job at Marco's. They closed down, went out of business. I'm looking for another waitress job, but, baby, they're not easy to get these days. Christ, he promises in endless prayers, if you'll just let me get out of here, I won't do another wrong thing. And I'll tell everyone I know how you saved me from hell. In his heart he feels better, believes his prayers will be answered. Perhaps, he thinks happily, I'll take up preaching in a tent.

He's afraid to close his eyes at night. The pungent scent of rubbing alcohol reminds him of death. The guy with no legs across the ward from him jerks off every night and giggles when he comes. The orderly is queer and has soft hands and offers Clyde certain relief if he wants with a lilting Southern voice. He says that he is from Alabama originally and is serving a stretch for violating morals laws. Whatever that means.

"All you'd have to do is just lay there," he says.

"Get the hell away from me!" Clyde seethes.

Once a week the doctor comes in with a fat nurse and makes his rounds.

"How's the foot?" he says.

"Hurts like hell."

"Sure it does. What'd you expect?"

The nurse smiles pleasantly. She'd be pretty if she lost some weight. She smells like Swanson soap. That night he fantasizes about her while the legless guy across the ward giggles.

The orderly says he heard through the grapevine that it was Chicago Willy who cut the kid's throat because the kid refused

18

to be his lover. Rolls his eyes and says, "His lover! What a hell of a thing to call it."

Bringing with the news is a peace offering of a couple of chocolate bars to which the orderly adds: "Hey, about the other night. I didn't mean no offense. Just that a lot of guys in here don't mind what I do for them, and I sure don't mind it either. But I understand how it ain't for everyone."

The chocolate bars are a real treat and he doesn't hold anything against the orderly, what is in his nature. A guy can't help what he is.

It's just life, you know.

And there in the sterile light of sheets like rows of the dead in a morgue, Clyde Barrow nibbles his chocolate and dreams of fast cars, guns, and Bonnie Parker.

2

Acts of Love

He kisses the tattoo above her right knee, just where tendon and muscle are strung taut under her ivory smooth skin, just at the narrowest point of her calf.

"Oh, my," he whispers, "would you just look at that."

"Do you like it, honey?"

"Like it!" He kisses it again, studying it like a map to some lost treasure.

Roy & Bonnie, set in double hearts, pierced by an arrow she paid a man five dollars to do with a vibrating needle that stung like little fire ants.

"You really love me, don't you, baby?"

"I really do, Roy."

Gosh, he was so big down there for not being all that tall. It sort of thrilled her in a way.

He had a habit of walking about the small apartment naked, forever wanting to make love to her. Horny as a goat he liked to say, and she loved it that he desired her so.

Texas wind riffles the curtains and blows warmly over their naked bodies. They sit cross-legged after making love for the second time and smoke cigarettes while he tells her of all his big dreams.

He tells her she is his Kewpie doll — this small happy doll with golden hair that glints red in the sun. He tells her how smart he thinks she is. She tells him she wants to be an actress or a singer. She tells him she is a poet. She has framed certificates from school of first place that she's won in spelling bees. He tells her he is lucky to have won her heart, such a smart pretty girl like her from such a nice family.

In her Big Chief notebook she writes poems. He likes one of her poems in particular: *Suicide Sal*. It's all about a gal and her beau and their tragic love — how the guy ends up throwing her over for another dame and the woman — Suicide Sal — kills them both. Roy doesn't plan on ever throwing Bonnie over for another dame, he promises her with a mocking smile.

"Kiss it again, Roy," she says. He feels himself stir when his lips touch the still healing tattoo, and she reaches for him and pulls him closer so she can press her lips to his.

21

"Boy, you're really something," he says as he feels her delicate little tongue dart in and out of his mouth as she's kissing him.

"I surely am," she says, and they make love again and fall asleep there in the middle of the day, her waitress uniform draped over the back of a chair, his shoes under the bed. He likes to say how they can really make the old springs squeak like banshees. But in their sleep, there is only the silence of a Texas summer to pursue their little snores.

Sometimes during their lovemaking, she has thoughts about the handsome postal worker who comes into the café every afternoon after his rounds and orders a slice of cherry pie and coffee and flirts a little with her. She almost wishes in those moments that she hadn't married Roy so early in life. Ted Hinton has a hell of a nice smile and the best manners you could want on a man. He isn't like some of the guys who come in and every chance they get pat her on the butt and say things like, "I'll bet we could sling some swell hash together, Bonnie." He isn't rude like that.

Most guys she ever meets only have one thing on their minds. Though she doesn't care half so much if they leave a decent tip — a quarter or fifty cents. It's like they're paying for her company in a way, it is like she is putting on a little performance for them and they pay her to watch. She even makes it a point to wiggle her hips at the really good tippers.

She wonders in those bliss-filled moments what it would be like to kiss the tall handsome Ted, to have him kiss her. Would he be a better kisser than Roy? Still, she isn't by nature the cheating kind. It is Roy she's had tattooed on her leg and Roy she'll stay loyal to as long as he is loyal to her. Still, a girl can dream a little, can't she?

And when they came and arrested Roy and put him away for five years, her mama said, "You ought to divorce him, Bonnie," but she said no.

"I'd feel dirty doing him that way, Mama."

Roy had given her a wedding band that she swore she'd wear till the day she died.

With Roy gone, a guy named Loneliness started coming 'round to visit. And a summer without love left her restless as a cat on hot pavement.

Her girlfriend Mary talks her into going out and having a few laughs and some drinks even though the hooch is illegal these days. They go to a blind pig Mary knows about in North Dallas. There are men at the club, plenty of good-looking

Joes just as lonely with some extra dough that they don't mind spending a little of on a swell-looking girl.

Guys with names like Eddy and Walt and Harry.

"Now all we need is every Tom and Dick," Mary says with a laugh when Harry, who says his last name is Bartholomew, introduces himself.

"Yeah, that's all we need," Harry says, never taking his eyes off Bonnie. "How about you and me taking a turn on the dance floor, kid?"

She dances with Harry. Harry holds her so tight she feels like a crushed flower in his strong arms. Later he gives them both a lift home in his Chrysler that is the color of cream.

"Like to see you again sometime soon, Bonnie," he says as they step out of the car, their heads light from the booze as they sway there on the sidewalk leading up to Mary's apartment.

"Sure," she says, because it's been nearly a year now since Roy went into the pen, and gives him her phone number there at Mary's where she's staying sometimes.

Next time it's just the two of them who go out dancing and after, on the way home, Harry parks under a big Dallas moon and runs his hands up under her skirt while they are kissing. The thrill of a guy's hands on her after nearly a year is too much to resist. Later she pulls on her nylons and fastens the tops to the snaps of her garter belt before lowering her skirt, feeling she's been dirty to Roy, but not so dirty as to say no when Harry asks if he can see her again.

Later, she lies in the small bed atop a crimson chenille spread and listens to "Falling in Love Again" and "Bye Bye Blues" on the radio. She listens to the soft patter of rain dripping outside the open window. She smokes and takes her notebook and in it writes a poem about a woman who has lost her sweetheart, not to prison, but to war. She thinks war is a much more romantic theme and imagines herself a war bride like Mary's aunt, Irma, was.

"My uncle Carl came home with gassed lungs," Mary told her one night when they came out of the movie theater after having watched *Morocco* with Gary Cooper and Marlene Dietrich. It was a balmy night and they stopped and got ice cream on the way home.

A war bride of a legionnaire would be romantic, Bonnie thinks as she begins to form the poem in her head.

But not a legionnaire who came home gassed and sickly. No, he would be a legionnaire that was tall and handsome and looked like Gary Cooper.

That's what I wish I were, she writes in her notebook.

It all makes her feel even more lonely, the rain and the songs on the radio and thinking about Roy off in the pen and what a crummy choice she made in marrying him.

God, she prays, I hope I find someone soon.

The days at Marco's Café are all the same, the work hard, endless it seems some days, especially breakfast and lunch hours. Her feet hurt from standing on them so much. Her legs hurt. Her lower back hurts. Ted Hinton comes in, orders pie and coffee, grins, chats. Bonnie waits for him to ask her out. He never does. He seems so shy she wonders if he's maybe religious or something. She realizes for all his good looks, he's not really the type of guy who would interest her. She prefers guys with an edge to them. *Bad boys,* her mama calls them.

"Not all of them," she argues.

Then one night she meets Clyde and she

knows Mama is right. There was ever a bad boy, it is Clyde Chestnut Barrow. He's got that look. Those dark secretive eyes that never look directly into yours. He has a pretty face and is about the same size as Roy, not overly tall, which would seem to fit well with her own petite frame she imagines were they to go out dancing together or making love. She likes his silk shirt and other fancy clothes. She likes that he wears kid gloves even though it is too warm to wear gloves.

"Hey," he says upon meeting her.

"Hey," she says back.

"I'm Clyde Barrow." Like that, like maybe she was supposed to have heard of him.

"I'm Bonnie Parker," she says with equanimity, her hands on her hips as much to show him what nice hips they are as to show him she's got a style all her own.

They both know that very instant it is something more than pure chance they have met.

He can't stop looking at her. She can't stop looking at him.

He takes his fedora off and turns it over in his hands smoothing its brim as he does. He's got thick dark hair she'd like to run her fingers through.

"So, you married or something?" he says, looking at the wedding band on her ring finger.

"Sort of," she says. "That a problem for you?"

"It's no problem for me. Is it a problem for you?"

"Not really. My husband is in prison. You might as well know the truth."

"Hey," he says, like he understands how a thing like that can be. "The truth is always best, right?" She doesn't believe he believes this.

She can't stop talking, can't stop telling him all her secrets, her history, everything about her she wants him to know because she knows she doesn't want anything between them from this moment on.

He listens attentively, like she always dreamed a guy would. He keeps saying, "Yeah, tell me more, Bonnie. I want to know everything."

Mary, who is with them that first time, asks do they want her to get them a drink or something. Clyde says, no, he doesn't drink booze.

"I could get us some Nehis," she offers, wishing a little she had spotted Clyde Barrow before Bonnie did. Both of them say no thanks.

Clyde offers to walk Bonnie down to the drugstore and buy her a Dr Pepper.

She feels safe on his arm. He walks on the outside nearest the street like a real gentleman. He wears his fedora at a cocky angle and tells her jokes that make her laugh and laugh.

He tells her how he's got big plans.

"Dallas is okay by me," he says, sipping his Dr Pepper through a straw there at the counter of the drugstore. Moths bat their wings against the window. "But I'd like to travel. You like to travel, Bonnie?"

"Sure," she says. "Who doesn't. I want to see the world. I'd like to see Morocco, places like that."

"Me too," he says, watching her fingering the little cross hanging on a gold chain at her throat.

"You religious?" he asks.

"No, just Catholic," she says. "What about you?"

He glances at the window, at the moths beating their wings against it.

"This husband of yours," Clyde says. "You planning on sticking with the guy till he gets out of the joint?"

She shrugs. "Maybe."

"Why would you stick with a guy who'd leave a sweetheart of a girl like you alone?"

29

He's a very perceptive guy, she thinks. He is looking at her now, waiting for an answer.

"That's a long story," she says.

"I got all evening," he says.

She lets herself fall hard for him, maybe too hard for just knowing him. He says he is crazy about her and is willing to do whatever it takes to prove it.

"I'll never leave you, Bonnie, if that's what you're worried about. The two of us would make a vow right here and now never to leave each other." She believes him. She wants to believe everything about him.

And even though he isn't a very good lover, it doesn't matter to her.

They lay in stony silence that first night and she thinks that the only reason he doesn't say anything is that he's embarrassed. She holds him, says, "It's alright, Clyde. None of it's that important. I just need to feel loved and cared about."

He tells her he's just got a lot on his mind right now, that next time will be better.

She's already making plans for the two of them in her head, already writing a poem about her and Clyde Barrow.

Then he goes and gets himself arrested

and thrown in jail. Only unlike Roy, Clyde escapes — simply walks away. But before he can get back to her, he gets captured again. The city of Waco seems timeless and distant on the dusty plains.

She tells herself to forget him in the time of her broken heart. It hurts and makes her angry.

Harry comes 'round but it isn't the same now that she's met Clyde. Harry's hands don't have the same allure to them anymore. His demeanor is so needy she could slap his face. She tries her best to forget love, forget that all men aren't created equal. She grows listless under the heat of his attention. She feels like a single bluebonnet smashed by the Texas sun, pulled by the Texas wind. Harry's breath is smelly with liquor, his tongue fat and rough.

"Hey, what's wrong, kiddo?"

"I am going to Waco," she says.

"Waco?"

"Something I have to do down there."

"You want, I'll drive you down," Harry says.

"No. I'm not sure I'm coming back. You better find yourself another girl."

His face crumples, looks like a wadded-up piece of her notebook paper — something with a bad poem written on it she has torn and squashed and thrown away. Too bad. Too bad. She has no sympathy for Harry.

Clyde's eyes light up like a pair of hundred-watt lightbulbs when he sees her there in the visitors room.

She confesses how she thought about not coming. Expresses her disappointment in him.

"You're turning out a lot like Roy did," she says.

"Ah, don't be like that, Bonnie. It's all a mistake they got me in here."

She wants badly to believe him. He was to tell her he's the pope, she'd want to believe him.

He has a plan for getting out.

"All you got to do is bring me a gun." The words slip from the side of his mouth like secrets of national importance.

She is squeamish about guns.

"I'd rather pick up a snake," she says.

He tells her he's got a friend who has a gun at this particular house. Explains how all she's got to do is go there in a taxicab, get the gun, sneak it back in to him, and he and the friend will be free . . .

"As birds," he says with a child's delight.

She knows before she leaves the jail that day she'll do it. She'll do anything for

Clyde Barrow. She doesn't know why, she just will.

The gun's blue steel is cold between her breasts tied there with a belt under her dress. It is not a big gun; it is just cold and heavy as a dead man's hand. By the time she arrives back at the jail, the steel has taken on the warmth of her flesh and she sort of likes the weight of it. A little ripple of something delicious travels down the length of her.

She likes it too when Clyde slips his hand down the top of her dress, the tips of his fingers stroking her breasts. She can't help but feel how tender and wanting he makes them before taking the gun out while his friend distracts the guard by asking for a light for his cigarette.

Clyde winks lewdly when he slips the gun into his pocket.

"Thanks, baby. Soon, it's just you and me — out there." He indicates with a nod of his head to beyond those walls of cement and steel — to the far-flung roads they'll cross and recross in a journey that has only one destination. He winks and touches her cheek and it feels like the wind coming through an open window of a Ford V-8. His farewell kiss seals the promise.

The next morning she hears on the radio how Clyde Barrow and his friend have broken jail.

She waits for him to come for her.

In her mind they are just actors in a movie, like Gary Cooper and Marlene Dietrich.

It is like a movie playing in her head, she writes.

3

Stealing Love's Beauty

She reads newspaper headlines.

CLYDE BARROW GANG STICKS UP GAS STATION IN HILLSBORO. ONE MAN SHOT. WITNESS MAKES POSITIVE ID. GANG ELUDES POLICE DRAGNET. DENTON JEWELER ROBBED — POLICE BELIEVE BARROW GANG RESPONSIBLE. BARROW GANG ROBS GRAPEVINE BANK.

Where is love in all this? she wonders.

Her tears fall faithlessly.

Even nights out at the movies can't stay the creeping dark dread.

Harry lights her cigarettes. Harry pats her hand. Harry makes love to her on cold moonless nights. She feels adrift, distant. She feels like the girl swinging on the moon.

Clyde is on the run. Clyde has guns and pals and probably molls too.

Bonnie paces and smokes and fills ashtrays with cigarettes whose tips are red with lipstick.

Why doesn't he call?

Then the cops come and arrest her.

"You helped him break out, sister."

"That's a good three to five."

Oh, God.

Handcuffs, police photographer's flash-bulbs like lightning bursts — "Turn to your left. Now turn to your right." Mug shots. Fingerprints. Delousing. Given a blanket, a pillow. She is put in a cell where something stirs — she is not alone.

The large, brutally built woman, who murdered her husband and children they say, watches her with mad eyes from under a blanket.

"Men," she mutters over and over again throughout the night.

In the shower where guards can watch her every move, Bonnie washes her waif-thin body quickly with a bar of hard soap as jokes are made, as nightsticks are slapped in the palms of hands. Sharing the shower with her is the murderess, her hair wet and stringy, chopped straight like a bowl-cut. Her chunky body, with its rolls of fat, look like an alien landscape. Bonnie Parker, Prisoner 188765, wonders briefly if the madwoman's poor husband did grow weary of the physical disorder, and was his little death a relief to him?

That night the woman utters the word "men" again before pressing her bulk against Bonnie, thereby pinning her to the cot, saying, "I only need to be held for a little while. It's been so long since anyone's held me."

In a hasty frightened prayer, Bonnie makes God promises she knows she cannot keep. The woman does not try and rape her, but merely lies like that holding Bonnie in her fat warm arms that eventually prove oddly soothing.

Bonnie's mother rides the bus down from Dallas to Waco, she says with the whine of a martyr, just to try to get her out on bail using grocery money she has been saving.

"Jesus, child. How did you let that little bastard get you in all this trouble?"

She can't explain it: the crazy things love for Clyde makes her do.

The charges against her are eventually dropped and beyond the ghostly image of her face in the bus's window, Bonnie watches the Texas countryside — its little gas stations and country stores she knows Clyde has no problem robbing. There is a grim beauty to it all — the grasses and bluebonnets and bedraggled small towns under a listless blue sky.

She writes a poem — "Blood & Bullets" — in her Big Chief notebook.

In it, she names Clyde, Jack, and the girl he loves, Sue, and tells how together they ride across the West in a fast V-8, robbing the rich and giving to the poor: a modern-day Robin Hood and Maid Marian. But like every poem she's ever written, this one has no good ending. For the lovers do die in a hail of "Blood & Bullets" and do lie slain in each other's arms.

Not long after she writes the poem Clyde is captured.

"Don't go to see him," her mother warns.

She vows she won't.

"We're finished," she tells her mother, her heart, God, anyone who will listen. She wants to believe it. She doesn't really.

The days again grow routine. She feels less joy now that Clyde has come and gone out of her life. The oaks do not surrender quite as much shade. The Dallas heat is immense and unkind. Even small children she sees in the park seem less happy. She often recalls the murderess's mad mutterings, the close, sickly sweat as she lay pressed to the billowy bosoms. Such memories knock at her heart's door like an unwanted Bible salesman.

Oh, never again will I do anything to

land in jail, she tells herself. *I'd rather be dead.*

Clyde writes her letters from prison.

Dear Bonnie, I love you . . .

Dear Clyde, I love you too, she writes in return.

At first she writes him letters every day. Then she writes only a couple of times a week. Later, whole weeks go by, sometimes a month or two where she does not write him at all. Still, his letters come regularly. She reads them, and puts them into a drawer beneath her nylons and underwear where they absorb the flowery scent from a tiny sack of potpourri she keeps there.

Ted Hinton still drops by Marco's Café and buys a cup of coffee and a slice of cherry pie every afternoon.

But Harry stops coming 'round to take her to the movies, dinner, dancing. He has obviously found a new love interest. Still, there are other men who end up taking her to such places, to hotel rooms full of street noises and minor complaints: men with mustaches and scars and crooked noses and big cocks and small cocks: men who drink and paw and cry out when they come. Men who tell her they love her, and those who don't. And in between the men are the days of standing on her feet, serving blue-plate specials, taking cigarette breaks, writing poems, dreaming of a someday-fame. And sometimes the days of sameness are so painful they feel like hammer blows to her skull.

A letter from Clyde arrives in the midst of her wanting to forget him.

I've got to get out of this place, he writes in desperation. His desperation is like that of a drowning child who is too far out in water too deep for anyone to save. And she feels in a way like the child's mother who is without arms or legs to swim. In a dream, she sees Clyde's fedora floating in a lake.

She thinks about going to California and becoming an actress. She's pretty and petite — the sort of girl who could catch the eye of a Hollywood director. She tells her mother of such plans.

"Don't be silly, Bonnie. You know you'd get homesick. You always get homesick." It is true. Home and Clyde Barrow are two things she can't stay away from very long.

Clyde writes and says his family is working to get his sentence commuted. Maybe in under a year he'll be paroled and they can be together again.

A year seems like forever. She tries not to think of how long a year really is.

She meets a guy named Glen who does

accounting for a bank. He looks a little like Gary Cooper, only not as tall and with darker hair.

Glen treats her swell, buys her flowers, candy, takes her to the movies.

She reads him her poems.

"Say, they're pretty good," he says with real enthusiasm.

He's so shy she aches for him to make a move. Their first kiss is gentle, unexpected, like the brush of a cat against your leg.

"Are you a virgin, Glen?" she asks him one sunny afternoon as they are having ice cream.

He blushes. She teases him about it. When they are almost finished with their ice cream he says he has been thinking about asking her to marry him. It is then she remembers that she is already married, a fact she has almost forgotten. Lost in all her loneliness is the fact that she has a husband.

Then there is that damn Clyde Barrow still fooling around with her heart even though he is up there in Huntsville Prison. He wrote just the other day to say he got his toes chopped off but doesn't mind because the food in the infirmary is better than in the regular prison and maybe being "a little mutilated" would help his case some.

Jesus, all of them? she wrote back.

No, just two, he wrote.

He said in the letter he thought when he got healed up, the missing toes wouldn't even cause him to limp and that he could still dance with her and get around normal. He never said if it was an accident or not. She was afraid to write and ask him more about it.

"Bonnie?" Glen says.

Lost in reverie, she comes back to Glen's question about her thoughts on his asking her to marry him.

"Ah, Glen, can't we just have a little fun for now?"

He tells her he is crazy about her. She knows he is like other men who were crazy about her. Sure, he says, whatever she wants. But he wants her to at least think about his proposal.

"Dance with me, Glen."

And so that evening they go and dance like little figurines on a music box, 'round and 'round, at one of the local clubs while the band played "Begin the Beguine." And later she and Glen go up to Glen's small apartment above a department store and drink a little illegal whiskey in their lemonades. Then she takes off her dress and drapes it across the back of the chair and stands in front of him in just her slip and nylons.

He sits on the edge of the bed and looks at her with the wondrous eyes of a child at Christmas.

"Glen," she says. And he raises his arms and she walks into them and his hands rest upon her slender hips.

"I've never had any real good luck with men," she says.

"I don't want to know," he says.

They kiss. She takes off his shirt. He holds her, his face pressed to her flat little tummy. She strokes his hair. He tells her he loves her. She knows it will probably be just this one night with him because he's grown so serious about her. But one night will have to do until she can decide what to do about Clyde Barrow, about Roy Thornton, about her entire stinking life and those who would steal from her love's beauty.

4

A Love Note

Clyde gets his parole. His foot still aches where toes should be. To make matters worse, the day of his freedom brings with it an ice storm that he rides from Huntsville to Dallas on a bus stinking with diesel. There in the back he smokes ready-mades, his right hand resting on a cardboard suitcase packed with everything he owns in the world.

The storm makes travel slow. Along the road, dumped in ditches, automobiles like black defunct beetles, folks standing by them scratching their heads. He sees frosty fields, barns and houses wearing sleet coats. He feels the cold sharpness of it down in his soul. His prison suit hangs loose on his shrunken frame from jail grub. He'd shoot a guy right now for a greasy burger. First thing he's going to do when he hits town is buy some new duds with his gate money: new hat, socks, shoes, underwear, everything. Buy a hot meal with coffee that doesn't taste like disinfectant. Eat slow and not have to worry about a knife in the back or some bull yelling at him.

Two years of his life down the drain. *No more,* he tells himself. *Next time it's all the way or nothing.* He feels old. He's only twenty-three.

The bus slides into Dallas, crosses the Houston Street viaduct that once was home — the very roof over the Barrow heads. He and his family lived below it for weeks when they first arrived from the Telleco cotton fields, what, ten years ago? The memory is like a photograph pressed to the back of his eyes. He remembers fighting with Buck and his sisters to see which of them got to sleep in the old Chevrolet sedan with the coughing motor and his folks who could be found in the front seat, sleeping propped up against each other. Him or Buck or one of the girls, there in the back, wrestling over the seat. Lying across that transmission hump was a bitch except on cold nights when the heat came up through the floor's rough nap carpet into your bones. But you ached like hell in the morning. Niggers didn't have it worse. He swore he'd never steal a Chevrolet. It was Fords or nothing at all.

45

And as if the world is glad to see him again, the sun suddenly breaks through and strikes the city a glancing blow setting it agleam, until it seems he's not entering Dallas at all, but paradise.

Glen sits with Bonnie on the old brown sofa in her mother's house listening to the radio: "Happy Days Are Here Again." Glen has been a steady suitor, his love and devotion steady. He is like the accountant of feelings, precise, aware, ready to dole out whatever Bonnie needs or wants in the way of love, affection, attention.

"Can I get you a glass of water?" "Do you want to go to the movies?" "Are you feeling okay?" "Have those headaches come back again?" Always ready to light her cigarette or help her on with her coat.

She should be grateful. He's a swell guy. Her mother says so. They smoke, listen to the music, make small talk. Her mother warns her about guys like Clyde Barrow, Roy Thornton, the others.

"Glen is sweet to you," her mother says. "Glen loves you, anybody can see that. You want to end up in jail again? You want me to have to bail you out of trouble again with the grocery money? Jeez, baby, you're so smart about everything but men. You should marry the guy."

"You forgetting, Mom, that I'm already a little married?"

"Then do yourself a favor and get a divorce."

She shrugs. Love has become a metaphor: the light at the end of the tunnel, the darkness underwater, the crooner invisible singing from inside the radio about a broken heart.

"It's that damn Clyde Barrow, isn't it?" Her mother is nervous, claims she can see the future — "And it ain't so good, Bonnie. Not if you're going to run with Clyde Barrow."

Suddenly the power goes out. The radio falls silent.

"Oh, not again," her mother says, coming in from the kitchen, wiping her hands on her apron.

They all just wait. In the silence they hear the ice crackling under the weight of the sun — a sound like a hammer striking glass.

Her mother goes to the window and looks out.

"The ice must have snapped the electric lines."

Glen pats Bonnie's hand.

47

"It's okay," he says.

"What's okay?" she says.

He prides himself in reading her mood. He doesn't know that he can't. Clyde and she could always read the other's mood as if they were inside each other's head. Clyde is a smart little guy for not having much education. Street smart and afraid of nothing. That is the thing that keeps Clyde at the very edge of her thinking, day and night. In or out of the arms of other men, at work at the café, while writing her poems, Clyde is always right there, popping into her thoughts. Just as right now, in the hasty silence, with the outside world coming undone, her thoughts are about Clyde Barrow.

And as if by magic there comes a knock at the door and when she opens it, Clyde is standing there under a cream-colored fedora. A cigarette dangles suavely from his lips, his hands stuffed into pockets against the icy air.

"Jesus," she says, her breath snatched from her chest.

"Got it wrong," he says. "Not Jesus, it's me, Clyde, remember?"

He looks scrawny; the pen stole some of him.

Behind her she can feel eyes: Glen's and her mother's.

"Well, you going to invite me in or do I have to stand out here freezing off what toes I got left?" His grin cuts through the veil of cigarette smoke. She is glad the pen didn't steal his sense of humor.

When she lets him come in, his gaze falls first on Glen, who stands impromptu as though about to greet a new business client instead of a rival. Then, as though he is unbothered by another man's presence, Clyde turns his attention to Mrs. Parker.

"Hello, Emma."

"Clyde," she says without a bit of warmth in her voice.

"Don't worry, I didn't escape. I got a pardon."

At this, he cuts his gaze back toward this guy who Bonnie introduces as Glen something or other, a last name that he immediately forgets because it isn't going to matter.

"Hello," says this Glen, a little officiously, extending a big smooth hand that Clyde can see right away has never done any hard labor. Clyde waits until Glen drops his hand back to his side. Then with measure, he turns again to Bonnie.

"Hey, kiddo, can we talk alone for a minute?"

She looks uncertain. He waits until she

says, "Sure," and takes him into the kitchen where he can smell something good in the oven: chicken and dumplings, maybe.

"Who's the guy?" Clyde says.

"Just a guy," she says.

"Just a guy, huh?"

"Yeah, what'd you expect, me to go fourteen years without anybody?"

She sees the sadness rain into his pretty brown eyes.

"He's just a friend, is all," she says, wanting to make up for any hurt inflicted, because she's been waiting so long for this minute, she is not sure how to handle it.

"We go to the movies sometimes, out to dinner, that's all."

"You expect me to believe that's all?"

"If you want," she says, "I'll go and get my diary and let you read it. You think that would make you feel better — knowing what happened every day you were gone these two years?"

"Can I at least get a little kiss?"

She feels all that pent-up anger, hurt, and loneliness in his kiss. It is like the tip of a knife pressed to her heart: cold and thrilling at the same time. She knows they've lost nothing for each other.

They hear Glen and her mother talking

out in the other room, Glen saying things like, "I don't understand, Mrs. Parker, who is this man?"

"I can't hang around Dallas long, Bonnie," Clyde says.

"You're leaving again? You just got home."

"I've got plans."

"I don't want you to be a thug."

"I'm no thug. I'm just a guy trying to make the best I can out of this lousy life."

In the other room they hear Bonnie's mother saying, "He's an old friend, that's all, Glen. Somebody from the past."

"Pack a bag," Clyde says.

"I just can't," she tells him. He kisses her again.

"Pack a bag."

While there in his embrace, she turns her head toward the living room. There is this swell guy Glen who treats her like gold, who wants to marry her, who has this honest job, who will never go to prison or be shot dead by the law. And then there is Clyde Barrow who most likely will — one, or the other.

"You go on to wherever it is you have to go and let me think about it a few days," she says.

"That's it then," he says. "You need time

to decide what you want, him" — nodding his head toward the other room — "or me."

He should have gone into performing mental tricks, she tells him, he's so good at reading people's minds. His lips purse in a moment's doubt before curling into a knowing smile.

She tries to explain to him life is more complicated now, that she is concerned about her mother, the same person "who got me out of jail after you got me put in, Clyde Barrow, lest you forget."

He looks abashed.

"Those days are over," he says.

She touches his cheek.

"They'll never be over, will they, sugar?"

"No," he says. "I don't guess they will."

In the depths of his eyes she sees long roads leading to nowhere. It is a journey she dreads, but one she can't resist.

"You got a choice," he says. "Me or this here. This what you want?"

She knows exactly what he means.

Then oddly enough, the electricity comes back on the minute Clyde Barrow walks out the door. Glen seems much relieved. Emma Parker seems much relieved.

Perhaps, Bonnie thinks with poetic remorse, the electricity went out so they could execute another guy up in Huntsville, and now that he's a goner, we all are back to normal.

And that very evening, after a long night of listening to the radio, and after which Bonnie's mother yawns and says how it's time she went to bed, Glen's advances are unwelcome, his hands pushed away, his murmurings of ardor deflected by the onset of feigned headache.

"What is it, Bonnie, what is wrong?"

She looks at him intently, there in the dim light from the floor lamp at the end of the sofa.

"You're a swell guy, Glen, but I don't see us as working out."

And thankfully he pretends he understands and without argument bids her good night. It is only while on his way home, with the bitter bile of regret pooling in his throat, that he is shattered when his automobile slips on a patch of black ice and slams into a telephone pole.

For Bonnie — when she hears the news the next morning on the radio — it is the last sure sign that she has made the exact right decision.

She packs a suitcase with all her red dresses and what few things she will need. She writes a note, tucks it in an envelope with her mother's name written on it, and leaves it on the kitchen counter. In it is a request, an extracted promise actually.

And when Emma rises and goes to fix her morning cup of coffee, and finds her name delicately written on the pink envelope, with fingers trembling she does retrieve the note.

And once read, she nearly faints.

If they kill me, Mama, don't let them take me to a funeral parlor. Love, Bonnie.

5

Faded Love

In a steaming bath of neck-high water, Ted Hinton rests, one arm dangling over the porcelain lip, fingers nearly touching the chair with Bible, bourbon glass, and application for the state police on it. His mind is giddy, or nearly so, with the prospects of a better job and the winsome waitress who serves him pie and coffee nearly every day of the week.

Oh, but a girl like Bonnie Parker would require someone much given to success, would she not? And what success is there truly in being a mail carrier? But the law! Well, the law is a horse of a different color. Everyone looks up to the law, the police, the gendarmes. There is power in the law, authority.

The whiskey settles like fire in his chest, pulls the shades of his eyes down slightly as he ponders a grand new future, perhaps a little cottage with a white picket fence, kids, a fine new automobile to drive around in. Walking for Ted Hinton has become tedious. And so too has the long loneliness that could be resolved by a girl so darling sweet as Bonnie Parker.

I could do some good, he thinks, being the law.

I could make a difference.

Texas is a lawless place, as lawless as any.

A man with a gun and badge could do some real damage.

Gunfights are played out on the backs of Ted's eyelids. Medals of valor are pinned to tan uniforms by grateful mayors. Headlines are written with his name emblazoned in large black letters. And maybe, every great once in a while, Pathé News will play a clip of his exploits between double features at the Bijou. *Texas lawman captures Pretty Boy Floyd in running gun battle!*

Oh, where is that damn pen? he muses, cutting a glance toward the application half filled out, and sees it lying on the floor, a drop of black ink clinging to its nib.

Then before he reaches it, he is again remembering the lithe little redhead in a crinkly uniform with a splatter of freckles across her pert nose. He has an abiding fondness for small women and imagines how young and tender would be her tiny breasts in his hands, were she to allow it. And maybe she would if he'd only work up the nerve to ask.

Steam rises from the bath like a swamp at night cooling. Trickles of sweat race down his sideburns. Is it the pen his hand is holding? Spasmodically he cools at last and drowses until the water forces him out.

Wrapped in a towel, he finishes filling out the application for the state police, hoping his feet have gone up the last sidewalk, his fingers have dropped the last letter into a slot of someone's front door. For what glory can be found in such tedious labor? What honor?

"This is Ralph Fults and Ray Hamilton," Clyde says by way of introduction when he pulls up to the bus station where Bonnie has stood waiting.

Both handsome boys, she has to admit, but are they going to . . . ?

"Chums of mine," Clyde says, but doesn't say right off chums from where.

Bonnie, for all her innocence in such things, is intuitive enough to know these chums have that look of men gone to prison and out again. Something motionless behind their eyes, like doors slammed shut so no light can ever get in again.

"How do," says Ralph, tipping his hat in a gentlemanly way. But the other guy, this Ray guy, only smiles like a wolf about to take a bite of lamb.

"Get in," says Clyde, popping open the passenger door as Ralph slips from the front seat to back alongside Ray.

Once in, Clyde gives her a peck on the cheek like she's his long-lost sister, then shifts and grinds the gears until they are moving down the street. The air inside the V-8 is full of gasoline and bay rum. Bonnie notices that Clyde's suit is new and crisp but that the other two have frayed cuffs and stained ties.

"Where are we going?" Bonnie asks her beloved Clyde, less sure now than she was fifteen minutes ago; the lie she penned to Mama still in her heart.

"Kaufman," Clyde says with a certain glee.

"What's there?"

"We'll find out when we get there, sugar."

Sun comes through the dusty windshield hot and bright as a furnace causing her to squint.

"You look good," Clyde says once they've cleared the Dallas city limits.

"Thanks," she says.

"Red looks good on you."

"It's my favorite color."

"I know. I don't forget anything you tell me."

One of the two in the backseat chuckles. She figures it is Ralph, the gentlemanly one.

Then for a long time they ride in silence under the veil of cigarette smoke and watch as the world outside the open windows seems heading the opposite direction, as though wanting to get out of the way of the coming storm that is Bonnie and Clyde.

After a flat tire and an overheated radiator they finally reach Kaufman as the last of the sun is bleeding into a pewter horizon. Shadows emerge and grow from the land. Darkness takes on its own form of life.

Shortly ahead their headlights strike a sign announcing a motor court — The Lone Star. A yard light shines brightly above the peak of the office throwing a circle of white upon the ground.

Ray and Ralph stand idly against the sedan, hands thrust down in their trouser pockets, while Clyde goes inside and rents two cabins. Emerging, he looks about as though scouting the lay of things — which of course he is — before handing Ralph a cabin key.

"The fellow inside says there is a place we can get grub up the road. Let's go eat, then turn in for the night."

"I thought we were going to . . ."

"Maybe after we eat, we'll look around," Clyde says, getting back behind the wheel.

It's two bits for a burger, ten cents for fried potatoes to go along with it, a nickel for a Dr Pepper, same for coffee. Pie is twenty cents. All out of the blue-plate special the waitress says.

"What was it?" Ralph Fults asks.

"What difference does it make, honey?"

"I'm just the curious type."

"Meat loaf, green beans cooked in bacon, and mashed potatoes."

"How much?"

"Seventy-five cents."

"Too bad you ain't got no more."

"Yeah, too bad we don't."

They eat, talk only enough to say, "Pass the salt, pass the ketchup." They wipe their mouths with paper napkins. They sip their coffee and Dr Peppers. They hardly look at each other. Bonnie desperately wants to be alone with Clyde. She touches his knee under the table. He doesn't say anything. She wonders why he doesn't.

After they eat they light up cigarettes and smoke and look out the window into the dark night. Bonnie begins a composition in her head about men smoking on dark empty nights — lonely men in cafés, perhaps searching for futures that don't exist. She thinks she might call it "Ode to Ex-Cons," or something dramatic.

"What do you think, Clyde?" Ray Hamilton says at last. It is the first he has spoken since Bonnie got into the car back in Dallas.

"It's going to be okay," he says.

"Yeah," says Ralph. "I think it will be too."

Bonnie wants to ask what's going to be okay but instead remains quiet. She wonders what her mother must be thinking since finding the note. She probably shouldn't have written what she did about dying and funeral parlors. God, what a terrible thing to tell her mother even though it remains her wish. She has heard tales about how they cut you up and take out your organs and pack you with sawdust. How they pluck out your eyes and put them in a jar and sew your eyelids shut. She does not want to be mutilated. She does not want her eyes in a jar.

Later back at the cabins, Clyde makes a futile attempt to consummate their reunion.

61

Crickets chorus somewhere within the room. Bonnie lies silently in his arms.

"You don't have to stay," he says after several minutes.

"You think that's all I want you for?" she says.

He shrugs.

"That's not what love is," she says.

"What is it then?"

"It's being with the person you want to be with — always. No matter what."

"Hell, I'm sorry I wasn't able to satisfy you. It's just I got a lot on my mind, you know."

"Give it time, sugar. You can. Just give it some time."

They breathe and do not speak for fear that the small intimacy building in them will shatter, will evaporate like fog against heat.

"We are lovers," Bonnie whispers.

Lovers, Clyde thinks and sees the broken body of a boy who refused such appellation.

"Forever and ever lovers," she says again and feels a slight tremble ripple under his skin.

Ted Hinton slides onto his favorite stool but is waited upon by a chubby brunette who has what appears to be a raisin under her right eye and asks what'll it be? He asks after Bonnie and is told Bonnie is no longer working here at this place.

Somehow the pie doesn't taste the same, the coffee not as good, and for the next several minutes, his time spent is just time spent and nothing special to it. Well, where did she go? he asks.

"I just started here today and don't know nothing about nobody," the raisin-eyed waitress says.

He thinks of his application to the state police resting in the bottom of his mailbag.

"Say, how do you like being a mailman?" the waitress asks, refilling his cup.

"It's okay," he says. "I'll be one for just another month or so."

"You leaving Dallas too?"

"I am going to join the state police."

"Oh," she says, then slides away, pot in hand, filling cups, Ted's gaze unwillingly following the shift of her broad hips even as he thinks that it is her lot in life to be of service to others. Ain't that what the Bible tells you?

Clyde says they are going to pull a job tonight. A hardware store, he says.

"But I don't want you having anything to do with it, Bonnie."

"Is that the way it is always going to be?" she asks, combing her hair.

"I was born to do what I do," he says. She sees the gun he slips into his pocket. "You were made to love me. That's what I want. I don't want you being some moll."

"Why'd you ask me to come if you don't want me?"

"You'll wait in the car, keep a lookout — that's all. Anything happens, drive away. Understood?"

"And if you're killed or something?"

"Then that's it."

She comes close, leans into him until her hand rests against the pocket with the gun that is hard and unforgiving to her touch.

"I'm either in it with you or I'm not," she says. "Whatever it takes, Clyde, I'm prepared for."

"You sure?"

"I want to live until I die," she says. "Don't you?"

"Nobody is getting out of this world alive."

"Then why are we discussing it?"

The way she says it arouses him. There on the unmade bed, morning light trying to slip between the cheap orange curtains, he takes her — shoves up the skirt of her jersey dress and enters her with his pants down around his ankles, the toes of his shoes dirtying the sheets in a way that leaves her smiling.

Emma Parker weeps and weeps for her delinquent daughter, the morbid words that flowed from her hand upon the note that spoke of dying and funerals.

Not my baby, she tells herself over and over. *Not my baby.*

6

Love's Razor

Bonnie watches from behind the steering wheel of Clyde's latest acquisition — a Ford V-8, forest green — three shadowy figures, Clyde and Ray and Ralph, pass under a streetlight. Watches a china-plate moon snagged in the branches of a tree.

Why does it take three men, she wonders, to rob a hardware store in that beyond midnight hour? Surely they aren't going to buy hammers and nails or paint. Before exiting, all three flashed revolvers — well, not flashed so much as took them out of pockets and spun 'round their cylinders and counted the number of bullets each had — then Clyde said, "Okay, let's go."

Clyde squeezed her knee, whispered, "You wait here, ready to drive in case it's needed."

She started to speak, but he threw her a look from behind the glow of his cigarette — a look that warned no debate was necessary.

Thirty minutes earlier she had been sleeping. Awakened by Clyde's urgent command to get up and get dressed, she did ask him what time it was to which he simply said, "Time to make a little moo-la-la."

It wasn't a dream she was having as much as it was a premonition when he'd awakened her; a thing with the weight of dread anchored to it. She'd been watching Clyde sitting on a rock, his hat cocked back, through the viewfinder of her Kodak saying, "Smile" and "Cheese" and "Your father's mustache" to get him to put a pleasant look on his face when suddenly blood dripped from his eyes.

Oh, how it frightened her.

But worse still was the feeling she had when awakened from dreams and dreads and all that. For she was sure someone had been watching her through an open window of the cabin. But when she went to it and looked out, all she saw was night, the rising moon. Clyde paced as she dressed and she thought he paced like a tiger caged.

She promised herself that when they returned to the cabins, she was going to check and see if there were footprints or a fresh cigarette butt there below the window. She did not like the feeling she

67

was having — the feeling about this place, these guys, Ray and Ralph — none of it, as she watched three shadows blend into shadow, as though all darkness were melting together to become one long night.

Clyde Barrow thinks to himself, *This is stupid.* Robbing a hardware store in the middle of the night has not to it the glory of the dashing Robin Hood Bonnie so often spoke about. But Ralph has sworn that this particular store has a fat safe full of thick green stacks of money that are only taken to the bank once a week on Friday afternoons, and this being Thursday night would be a prime opportunity to pull an "easy job."

Oh, well. Oh, well. What difference does it truly make whether you take down a bank or a hardware store? Money is money. People do not ask, "Where'd this come from?" when you hand it to them for a new shirt, a hamburger, gasoline. No they do not ask and are glad to get their hands on it.

And so stealthily he creeps along with Ray and Ralph onward, gun in hand just in case something goes awry and they have to do some shooting, which he is not opposed to if necessary. And necessary it may be if the cops come or someone else who opposes such plans as are in his head. For he's vowed that very day when he saw the kid lying in the swirling pink waters of his own blood flowing down the prison shower drain that he would never go back to jail again. Dead is better, he told himself as they break the lock on the back door and creep in.

Oh, it is dark in this place. Dark and dry and smelling of metal screws and wood and all things uninteresting to a Robin Hood. And stumbling around in the dark while searching for a safe that does not exist except in the mind of Ray Fults, an alarm sounds from somewhere outside.

An old man who lives across the street from where the stolen Ford is parked with Bonnie in it saw the trio skulking toward the store and phoned the police. The wail of the police car siren as it rushes out of farther darkness toward the store sends hearts racing and three men out again into the night dashing toward the waiting car.

"Drive, drive!" Clyde shouts, but does not wait for Bonnie to even turn the key before shoving her aside and taking the task into his own shaking hands. And off they go, pell-mell through the little town of Kaufman that just hours earlier looked so full of promise, so fat with easy money.

Clyde drives, it seems, without letup until the dawn comes creeping over the horizon — the sun like a sleepless eye opened to keep watch at their coming. And when the fury and fear are all fled, Clyde pulls into a grove of trees — cottonwoods would be the correct name — and turns the engine off.

"Well, that was some heist," he says, angrily at first. Then his bitter-set mouth curls into a wry grin.

"Thought you said there was a safe in there," Ray says to Ralph, unamusedly.

"Supposed to be," Ralph says.

"Well, there wasn't any safe I could see. You see any safe in there, Clyde?"

Clyde does not answer, but instead stands and watches as the sun catches fire in the little creek that flows between the trees as they get out to stretch their legs and Bonnie goes off toward some privacy — the ache in her bladder intense.

"What now?" Ray says to Clyde who stands pissing toward the east.

"Well, we go back to Dallas," Clyde says. "I'm taking Bonnie back to her mother's. I don't want her caught up in all this business.

I don't want her shot or killed or jailed."

"But what about after? What's the plan?"

"I'm thinking," Clyde says, zipping up his trousers — his work here in this place all done.

"Some gang we're supposed to be," are Ray's final comments on the subject as he watches the lovely young woman return from her privacy. *Oh, I could do that some real good,* he thinks. *I know old Clyde ain't doing the job. Not from the way I heard how he got to like it in prison.*

It is no trick for Bonnie to read Ray Hamilton's thoughts. His eyes tell the same story a hundred other men's eyes have told her. Clyde stands leaning against the front fender of the Ford smoking a cigarette, no doubt adrift in bandit thoughts.

If she could just love him enough, she thinks, he would find a different occupation. All a fella really needs in life is enough love to change him around.

She comes up and puts her arm around him boldly so that Ray can see whose woman she is, And then notices how those slate gray bandit eyes drift over her with a sexual malice she has known before and feels somewhat ashamed because it thrills her slightly too.

When Clyde stops the car again he says: "I'll come back for you in a few weeks." She touches his face. She makes him promise, right there in front of Ray and Ralph. He promises he will.

She can hear Ray and Ralph in the backseat breathing through their noses.

She can smell their sweat and the upholstery and burnt oil.

She can feel the heat coming up through the floorboards, through the soles of her pretty red shoes.

"Don't forget your suitcase," Clyde says, then drives off.

Her mama weeps crazy tears to see her again.

And she weeps crazy tears of longing for Clyde.

"I tried to tell you he was no good for you, Bonnie."

She goes to her old room and lies down on the bed and stares at the ceiling, the cracked places in the plaster, the plain curtained windows, until her eyes blur with the same crazy tears.

She writes in her notebook: *Will true love ever find me?*

Clyde feels lonesome and mean and

hungry for something.

He and Ray and Ralph drive to Fort Worth, Ray saying how much he could use a woman. His head is still full of thoughts of how much good he could do a girl like Bonnie Parker. Maybe if things work out, he'll sneak back and see her.

Ralph says he knows of a whorehouse there in Forth Worth.

"Yeah, like you knew about that safe in Kaufman, right?"

"No, this place I been to. I know the score."

"They got any redheads there?"

"Sure, I guess. I guess they got whatever a guy is looking for. Least they did last time I was there. I'm partial to platinums."

And afterward, after they go to this whorehouse where Clyde waits in the car for them, Ray wants to get some gin to drink.

"I don't drink," Clyde says.

"You don't do much," Ray says.

"What's that supposed to mean?"

"It don't mean nothing."

And the night comes down on them.

Bonnie tries to count the stars wondering which star Clyde is standing under just then and throws off her clothes in a tantrum of frustration. Oh, what is it he doesn't like well enough to take her with him? *This?* She touches each pear-sized breast. *This?* Her hand wanders lower to the sandy thatch between her legs.

But no, Clyde has said he loves her well enough. All of her. And touches and kisses her every place and lets his gaze fall over her like night on water. His eyes like stars.

And it is a restless, dream-filled sleep she falls into eventually. But in the dream Clyde is nowhere present. There are just black cats and a stranger who steps out of the shadows and says his name is Ray Hamilton.

"Ex-con," he says.

"All man," he says.

And stretches forth his hand.

Clyde grits his teeth in his sleep.

The sharp edge of a razor touches his throat like a hot wire.

"Bonnie!" he cries out, rousting Ray from his impure thoughts.

But Ralph sleeps like a baby.

7

Love's Highways

For days she writes poems, listens to the radio, argues and laughs with her mama. A letter arrives from Roy, which she reads and tears up and does not bother to answer. In it he says he hopes to get out soon and how much he misses her. Roy is yesterday's news as far as she is concerned. Her mama asks again why she just doesn't go ahead and file for a divorce.

"I don't know," she says. "I just haven't."

Her mama's feet swell. Bonnie fixes her ice baths to soak them in. They smoke and talk endlessly. Bonnie reads the newspapers for word of Clyde's activities. She reads where a gas station was robbed over in Denton but all it says is: ASSAILANTS UNKNOWN and that less than a hundred dollars was stolen along with some tires and gasoline. It further says: GUNSHOTS EXCHANGED, NO ONE HURT.

For this she is grateful. So many bad

dreams about Clyde have made her wary.

She reads of a woman raped in Sulphur Springs by two men, but she knows it wasn't Clyde for lots of reasons.

It rains for three days and nights running. Hard windy rain that raises a staccato along the eaves, that pings against the windows and dances down the streets. The rain makes everything feel less bearable, makes sad songs on the radio sadder, makes the days longer, the nights longer.

She calls her friend Mary out of dopey desperation, out of irrepressible boredom.

Mary's voice lilts and tilts like a pinball machine. Bonnie sees the colors of Mary's voice in her head.

"Hey, I didn't know you were back. You and Clyde split up?"

"I'm just back for a little while."

"What about Clyde?"

"Returning soon."

They make plans to go out.

"Just a movie," Bonnie makes her promise. "No men or nothing."

"Sure, whatever. All this rain is depressing, ain't it?"

Meantime lightning jumps out of the sky with amazing savage grace — jumps out of dark brooding clouds with the suddenness of a snake strike. Ralph wanders off alone, as though drawn by the snake strike lightning.

"Where'd he go?" Clyde asks, shaken awake by thunderclaps in the single motor cottage room they all rented together.

"Hell if I know," Ray says, scratching himself on the other bed. "Hell if I care." For in Ray's way of thinking, money split two ways adds up better than split three.

It is sometime the following morning they hear on the radio a man has been caught trying to steal a car. The man as described sounds a lot like Ralph.

"The dope's been caught," Ray says cockily.

"We better scram out of here."

And so they drive aimlessly until Ray says he remembers hearing while in the pen of a grocer over in Hillsboro who also runs a little pawnshop.

"I'm tired of small potatoes." Clyde yawns at the breaking dawn.

"This old boy keeps a box of gold watches, diamond rings, you name it. Pistols, too."

"All we'll probably end up stealing is a loaf of bread if it was like that last job."

"You know if he's got watches and rings, he's got plenty of cash to buy them with."

"If!" Clyde says with a certain disdain. "That's a big word sometimes."

But Ray can see with morning sun seeping through the windshield that he has whetted Clyde's appetite. Can see the way he grips the steering wheel with both hands and floors the gas pedal until it feels like the V-8 is going to shake apart running down those rutted Texas back roads.

Billy Dash wears his hair slicked back. Wears white on white silk shirts and gold cuff links. Wears Italian ties. Wears black and white shoes. Billy Dash is small and ferretlike. A slick little weasel.

Billy Dash owns a gin joint just off Houston Street where you can buy illegal booze or girls. He keeps a dice pad, a couple of poker tables. Takes side action, front action, any kind of action. Billy Dash has his fingers in many illegally baked pies.

Billy Dash has cops and politicians and judges for friends. Billy Dash keeps his money folded in a silver money clip of his right-hand trouser pocket, which he sometimes pulls out with manicured fingernails.

Mary says she knows this blind pig they can stop off at when they walk out of the movie theater that evening. It is a cool damp night, heavy with the feel of lonely to it. Rainwater stands slick and shining in the streets. The air tastes clean. The stormy evening sky is a faded shade of muted red.

"No, let's just go home," Bonnie says, but only halfheartedly. Clyde's been all over her mind. She's been having this really dark feeling about him.

"We could maybe meet some nice guys," Mary suggests.

"I'm not interested in meeting any nice guys."

"Okay, so we just stop and have one teensy drink. What's the harm? Jeez."

So as not to create a stir, Bonnie allows herself to go along up Houston Street, up a back stairway where yellow light falls out of second-story windows like melted butter. They come to a landing, Mary knocking on the door twice. After the second knock, somebody inside slides back a peephole and then a lock and lets them in.

Music and laughter rush out like gleeful wraiths to greet them. Once inside through the smoky blindness of cigars and cigarettes, eyes follow the swing of their hips, the bounce of their breasts. Billy Dash comes forth to personally introduce himself.

"Ladies."

Billy Dash, Bonnie notices, is wall-eyed. He introduces himself with an oily gesture of smoothing first the side of his hair before extending the same hand to each of them.

"This is Bonnie and I'm Mary," Mary says mirthfully, taking his hand in hers that Billy kisses the knuckles of, the overhead light running through his hair like electricity.

And when he tries the same with Bonnie she makes sure to retrieve her hand before he can wetly kiss it, turning her attention instead to the roomful of partiers, saying, "Mary tells me a girl can get herself a teensy drink in this place."

"Indeed, indeed," Billy says with nary a hint he's been much offended by this standoffish, pert young woman of whom he'd like to know more in intimate detail. He's known her type before and takes her rebuff as a personal challenge. Win her over, then most likely as not once he's had his way with her, somewhere down the line throw her out like yesterday's fish.

Oh, how Billy Dash does like a challenge. For this girl called Bonnie he's got plans.

And while Billy Dash is making his plans, Clyde and Ray are making theirs.

They sit patiently smoking cigarettes across the street from the grocer's store. They wait and wait and wait until they see the last light go out in an upstairs room.

And when it does, Clyde says, "Let's go."

After knocking hard several times they hear someone lean out the window and call down on them.

"We're closed," a man's voice says. "Come 'round tomorrow."

"Just need to pawn my watch, mister. We're flat broke and got no money for gas to get back to Dallas. My wife's real sick."

A woman's voice is mutely heard before the man says, "All right, all right. Hold on."

And in a moment, he does let them enter, dressed as he is in a red-checked robe tied 'round his middle, his manner that of a man who has trusted friends and strangers all his life. Clyde lays the cheap watch on the counter and says, "How much can you loan on this?"

"Why," says the man after holding it up to the light, "it's an Elgin, and not a very expensive one at that. I guess I could go two dollars."

"Not enough," Ray says and shows the man his black gun.

The woman appears from the shadow of the stairwell.

"John, what do these men want?"

"I guess everything we got," the man

says as Ray nudges the barrel of his gun into the man's ribs.

"Oh, dear God!"

"Hush, hush now, lady," Clyde urges. "Let's you and me stand back here and let my partner do his business, then we'll be on our way and you'll never even know we were here." She is plump like a hen.

There is some debate between the man and Ray.

"We don't have much."

"You've got more than us."

"Please don't hurt us. Don't hurt my wife."

"We ain't going to hurt nobody. Open that damn safe."

The man kneels before Ray like a supplicant. Kneels before the barrel of Ray's gun. His hands shake terribly. Ray tells him to calm down.

The first few tries at opening the safe fail. Ray grows anxious. Clyde grows anxious. The woman starts to chitter, her false teeth click inside her mouth.

"Easy," Clyde cautions. Then to Ray: "Hurry it up."

"I'm trying, goddamn it."

Nudges the pistol barrel against the man's temple.

Then suddenly the right combination is

struck and in the rush of relief, as the man swings open the little safe's door, it knocks against the pistol that then goes off with an explosion that is shocking. Loud as a stick of dynamite. And without a single word the man topples face forward.

Clyde feels the missus sag, tries to hold her up, but her weight takes her down to her knees. Clyde feels helpless. Feels a hot anger.

"What the fuck did you do?"

Ray looks blankly at the man, at the open safe, at Clyde. His pistol breathes smoke.

A gasp emits from the dying man. A single gurgle. Then nothing.

Then they hear a siren.

Only it's not a siren, but the wailing of the grieving woman.

Ray is grabbing everything he can from the safe, blood pooling 'round his shoes, coming up through the hole in one sole, soaking into his sock so his toe feels the warm stickiness.

Racing off into another Texas night, Clyde says, "You just turned us into murderers."

"He killed himself," Ray says, trying hard to light a cigarette.

"No, you killed him. And I was with you. And the way the laws will see it is we both killed him and when they catch us, they'll put us in the chair."

"They ain't going to catch me!" Ray says, opening the wing so the cool air can rush in over his hands and face.

"They ain't going to catch me either," Clyde says. "And if they do, they ain't going to take me alive."

"Shit," Ray says. "Me either."

And while the grocer struggles toward the white light awaiting him at the far end of a tunnel he's never seen before, Billy Dash does confide to a confidant, a rugged bulk of a man who maintains order with fists and fury: "That dame dancing with that other dame — the little strawberry blond. Make sure she comes see me in my office before she goes."

But Bonnie is alert to such ruses. Clyde has taught her to be observant. She turns to Mary and says, "Let's go powder our noses." And later, having slipped out a lavatory window onto a fire escape and down an alley, Bonnie feels she's breathing for the first time in an hour.

"We could have stayed around and had some laughs." Mary is more than a little disappointed in Bonnie's skittish behavior, was hoping to maybe meet a nice guy or two before the evening did end.

"We would have been raped, maybe our throats slit afterward," Bonnie says, hurrying along, the rain again dripping from the blood-burst sky.

"Aw, you're cuckoo."

And later, in bed alone, her mother asleep on the sofa when she first came in and asleep still, Bonnie shakes from the fear of what might have been.

She smokes a cigarette in the naked dark. Her heart thumps under her ribs. She wishes Clyde were here to hold her, to protect her from rabid men.

So when the next morning he is standing there at her door and sees in his eyes the same loneliness and fear she's been carrying in her, she slips upstairs and takes the bag she's packed already and bids silent farewell to sleeping Mama.

Ray Hamilton is there in the backseat, bunched up under his suit jacket, hat pulled down over his face. Bonnie smells the whiskey on his somnolent breath as Clyde throws the bag in the trunk.

"Do we have to take him?"

Clyde peers in at the now killer, the one who has turned him into a killer as well.

"We . . ." he starts to explain. "Oh,

just get in, will you."

But she does not get in.

"What is it?" he says.

She looks into that haggard face, so young, yet so old suddenly.

"I missed you," she says.

Then like that, he takes hold of her and kisses her so tenderly she knows that whatever is waiting for them, no matter how many are their days yet to come, she's never going to leave him. She's never going to let him leave her.

"It's just us," she says. "From now on it's just always going to be us."

The light is golden that morning, as though the storms of the previous three days and nights did wash away some buried treasure of a sun. And the golden light falls upon the face of Clyde Barrow, the rough growth of unshaved beard, the disarray of hair falling from under his gray fedora and shagging across his eyes.

"That's it, sugar. It's just us, all the way. We're all we've got."

He holds open the passenger door like a true gentleman, like a lover. She pauses before getting in.

"I don't care," she says.

"You don't care about what?"

"I don't care what happens."

"You sure?"

"Let's just live until we die."

His lip curls back in a wry but very sad way.

"Maybe that will be a long time from now," he says.

"Maybe forever."

Mother Emma watches the reunion from behind a rain-washed window and feels the bottom go out of her heart.

There on the kitchen table another note: a lie, pure and simple, she knows this time. She reads it briefly, knowing the lie is at hand — this daughter telling of a job in Houston as a manicurist.

Oh, goddamn you, Clyde Barrow, for stealing her from me again.

8

Love's Moment Stolen

Apple trees stand under the morning haze like old Rebels who have stopped to rest on some long journey homeward. Bonnie's imagination catches fire at seeing them. She likes to look with eyes unfocused at the world around her.

"They look like old soldiers," she says.

Clyde asks who looks like old soldiers.

"Those trees in the orchard."

He looks but sees only trees, their fruit unripened. Recalls the times as a boy he and his folks picked about everything a farmer could grow: cotton, lettuce, pears, peaches, and apples too. The work was achingly hard for so little money. He hates anything with that much work strung to it.

Ray Hamilton mutters something from the backseat, sits up, looks around, asks, "Where the hell we at?"

"Oklahoma, I do believe," Clyde replies through the smoke of his cigarette.

"I'm about starved out of my skull," Ray grumbles.

For once, Bonnie is in agreement with the man with hungry eyes.

The road they are driving cuts a dusty swath between the many orchards but eventually does come to one that is tarred. Clyde pauses at the intersection, looks at Bonnie.

"Which way, sugar?" he says, and she thumbs right to which he turns the wheel, heading in the direction from which the sun will eventually rise and burn off the haze.

They eat in a café full of farmers whose bulk fills faded denim coveralls and worn-thin cotton shirts, whose heads are bare. A hat tree full of caps stands in the corner. Bonnie thinks of the caps as eviscerated fruit hanging from a dead plant — the fruit mostly dirty green or gray.

The farmers watch the trio with the vested interest community has in strangers.

At midpoint of the meal, Ray asks the waitress where the toilet is and she tells him outside, 'round back, to which he rises and goes.

"I'd like for us to drop Ray off somewhere soon as we can," Bonnie requests of Clyde.

He is chewing a thick piece of bacon. His lips are wet and shiny from the grease.

"I need him to do my work with," Clyde replies.

"He gives me the heebie-jeebies."

"How so?"

"The way he's always looking at me."

"He won't bother you. He knows better."

"Says you."

Clyde pauses in his chewing, a fork in one hand, its tines pointed toward the stamped ceiling. A green-headed housefly, or horsefly, maneuvers around the lip of Clyde's coffee cup.

"He put his hands on you or something?"

"No."

"He say anything dirty to you?"

"No, Clyde, he never has."

His jaw moves. His teeth grind. He swallows the last bit of bacon.

"If he ever does, you'd tell me, right?"

"I'm telling you now, I don't like the guy."

Clyde reaches for the cup, the fly takes wing.

"Couple of more jobs, is all," he says after sipping the now-tepid coffee. "Then I'll cut him loose. That okay?"

Bonnie sees beyond Clyde's shoulder a thick-skulled farmer with a baked-red face staring at her. If she unfocuses her eyes just enough, he looks like a pink hog.

"Say, sister," Ray asks the waitress upon his return, drops of water strung through his hair. "How far to the nearest town?"

The waitress's own hair is the color of lead, her face puffy with age and weariness. She has broken veins in her thick legs. Bonnie is truly grateful she is with Clyde and not still working at Marco's Café, or some joint just like it. In the waitress, Bonnie sees a future she does not want.

"Stringtown's about thirty miles up the road, if by town you mean a place that has most things a body could want."

"They have a dance hall?"

"They used to. Lord, I've not been to a dance in ten years."

Then as though they hadn't been speaking at all, Ray turns his attention from the waitress to the last of the scrambled eggs on his plate shaking on still more pepper. And when finished says to Clyde, "I'd like to shake a leg tonight at that dance hall."

Bonnie is surprised when Clyde agrees, his mood suddenly almost buoyant.

"Yeah, maybe we could all use a little fun," he says.

And so do kill the remainder of the day resting amid an orchard just outside of Stringtown, having earlier crossed the Red River to which Clyde did say, "It don't look any more red to me than any other river, does it to you?"

They spread blankets on the grass in the shade of the gnarly apple tree branches. The scent of sweetness is in the air, as though the marble-sized fruit are releasing their wondrous essence for the world to behold. Bees buzz in the sweet air.

Bonnie sits with her legs across Clyde's while he rubs her feet.

"They're so small, your feet are," he says.

"Petite," she corrects.

"Petite," he says.

Ray walks around looking at the trees as though some official inspector of apple trees. They all look the same to him.

They languish. They doze. They talk. They smoke. They make plans. Explore possibilities. They hear trucks and automobiles pass along the road in the distance. Once they hear deep-throated laughter from a passing truck with several men standing in the back.

Twice, Bonnie catches Ray watching her

as he leans on one elbow from a nearby blanket, a stem of grass between his teeth. She thinks the stem of grass could easily be one of her small bones he is sucking the marrow from. The feeling it gives her is like a drop of ice in her blood.

The second time she catches him watching her — Clyde asleep on his belly, his hat over his face — Ray looks at her, then off farther into the orchard. A gesture she understands very well. She glares at him, hoping he is not too dense to realize she won't go off with him farther into the orchard. He simply twists his mouth into a crude smile, a pucker of sorts that shows his front teeth as a slight wind does come and riffle his pretty golden hair.

Bonnie has a moment of dreadful thought: Ray is dangerously handsome.

With the sun leaning in the west, Bonnie tells Clyde she wants to go wade in the Red River.

He gives it some thought, calculates the distance in his head to how far back the Red River is.

"Aw . . ." he starts to say, but then sees her keen wanting.

"What the hell. The sun won't go down for three more hours." Thinking of the dance in Stringtown that evening.

Ray is not so thrilled about tracking back the way they came.

"Why didn't we just stop when we got to it, if that's what you wanted to do?"

But Clyde is already getting in behind the wheel. Ray knows that is how Clyde is: impetuous. Like an energetic child.

The water is colder than Bonnie had expected, even soaked with late-afternoon sun.

Little goose bumps run up her legs.

Clyde stands with his trousers rolled up, his jacket off, his fedora pushed back on his head.

Ray refuses to go anywhere near the Red River. Even at Clyde's cajoling.

"I can't swim."

"It's not deep unless you keep going out."

"I could step in a damn hole or something."

"Quicksand too," Clyde says. "I hear these rivers are full of quicksand. I read when I was a kid how cowboys would take cattle drives across this river and they'd get down in the quicksand and that would be the end of all of 'em. This river is full of cowboy bones, I bet."

Ray shudders, lights another cigarette, says, "You go on and drown if you want to

— me, I'm staying right here."

Bonnie is more daring, wades out until the water is lapping her thighs, her skirt gathered up in her hands.

"It's not so cold once you get used to it," she calls to Clyde.

"I've gone about as far as I want to," he replies, thinking of that damn quicksand. It was the Red River he'd read about as a kid, wasn't it? His foot touches something hard and smooth he cannot see. A cowboy's bone?

Ray does watch the slender bare legs of Bonnie Parker as she explores with gleeful trepidation the river's shape. Does sigh and wonder at what pleasures such slender limbs might give a man. Does feel a need to go off farther into the orchard alone, knowing Bonnie will not accompany him, and satisfy an urge newly risen, but old as man itself.

Three hundred miles from the Red River — rising from his bed — Ted Hinton tries hard to hold on to the dream. Her name is Bonnie Parker, and in the dream, she and Ted were picnicking. And they had children — several — and Bonnie was laughing and saying how happy she was to be married to him. And oh how happy he too was until the dream broke.

Ted Hinton coughs up the phlegm of last night's cigarettes.

Well, at least I do not have to carry the mail today, he reminds himself.

Today he is to shoot pistols and learn the law.

He finds himself feeling happy between the dream and his new job.

He yawns and stretches. He does his best to ignore his dream-swollen penis.

God would not want me lusting after her, he tells himself on the way to the bathroom to shave and get ready to shoot a gun and learn the law.

But still . . .

The sky turns crimson, tatted with a lace of clouds. Then at the blue-black edges does appear a crescent moon. Then, does appear the Dog Star. That's all there is — Clyde thinks, looking at the lonely symbols — besides somebody's idea of heaven, as he waits for Bonnie to change her dress behind the privacy of the Ford V-8.

And soon enough they do find the dance in Stringtown under a large tent big as a barn with electric lights and music. Automobiles parked on the grass. Men and women strolling arm in arm toward the dance floor, toward the small band of five men in shirtsleeves with guitars and fiddles and one slapping a bass.

"Well, hell, I'd say we're in for a good time," Ray Hamilton says with glee.

"You best be careful, old son," Clyde replies.

"You hadn't ought to deny a man his pleasure. After all, you got Bonnie."

"All I'm saying is . . ."

But Ray is busy drinking some whiskey from a Mason jar and already about slop drunk. Clyde sees the glitter in his eyes as Ray exits the car, the jar still in his hand.

Oh, the rush and crush of bodies as they all do dance upon the sawdust floor, the music falling down on them like hot rain, the sound of shuffling feet, the warmth of flesh so prevalent pressed there on that warm August night.

Ray is dancing with an auburn-haired woman with large hips and taller by a head than he.

Bonnie says, "This would be a prime opportunity to hit the road — just the two of us. Ray can make his way on his own."

Clyde is awkward, steps on her toes.

There comes a break, the musicians trailing outside to catch some air, perhaps a little refreshment from the large metal tub of lemonade.

There is the buzz of elated voices ripe with the night's activities. Men knowing that the better they behave, the more grand they strut, the more likely the reward when they get home again. Women with hearts alive from this rare opportunity to forget their woes and daily drudgeries, to don fresh dresses and paint their lips and once again feel desirable. A few children scurry about wildly. Men lean on automobiles and smoke and women head off for the privies together.

Ray is fully engaged in conversation with the tall woman, sipping his shine as he does from the Mason jar when two men do approach and start to say, "Hey, that's illegal," their badges catching some of the electric light from bare bulbs strung overhead. They are not even in uniform, just bib overalls with badges pinned to their shirts. Pistol belts.

Ray fires his gun twice. Then fires twice more.

The happy little world breaks apart. Is shattered by the heartless act.

Clyde is pushing Bonnie toward the stolen auto.

"Run, run!"

Even as the crack of pistol shots does echo up into the lovely little night.

Even as good folks do drop to their knees, do cover their heads, do scream and scream.

Even as Ray is running, firing his gun over his shoulder that has left in his wake two officers of the former peace — one dead, the other possibly dying.

"Oh, Jesus Christ," Clyde is yelling as he turns the ignition and tromps the gas pedal hard enough the rear wheels send a spray of rock and dust toward the cowering crowd.

"Oh, Jesus Christ. Oh, Jesus Christ!"

And the dirty black night does accept them as one of its own, it seems.

9

Love's Labor Lost

If an artist, say, were on a journey to paint images of the rural Southwest, and were to pause there by the road where a strand of rusty fence wire ran the length of the weed-choked ditch and looked beyond it to the unmown fields, to the sagging old buildings that once held corn and tools and possibly cattle, he would have noticed a small white farmhouse, nondescript. And upon further study, he would have seen the blistering paint of the house's weathered boards, the busted lower step of the porch, the shades of the windows all pulled down, green and taut.

And when he'd finished his respite, most likely the supposed artist would have continued his journey in search of something more artistically pleasing than that simple little house. He would have perhaps sought something in the nature of an old plow left lying on its side, or a brightly painted red water pump, or chickens strutting in a yard. He would not have been aware that inside the farmhouse three people whose blood still vibrated with the sound of gunfire slept like children.

Bonnie lay curled against Clyde in a bedroom growing dense with summer heat.

And the artist could not have known about the killer, Ray Hamilton, stretched out on a gray sofa in hazy bliss with an empty Mason jar near his silent fingers.

Nor would our artist have seen the many pistols and automatic rifles that lay scattered about in strategic positions.

And lastly the curious artist would not have seen that everyone except Bonnie Parker slept with shoes on. Like tramps often did.

In a house not too dissimilar, but quite some distance away, sits a woman, nay, a widow, who is having trouble adjusting to her new status. For it seems to her that her husband, E.C., is just out there somewhere and will come walking in any moment and relieve her of her grief.

But in the marrow of her heart she knows this will not happen. For she did see him the evening before in the funeral parlor, in a room sickly sweet from many baskets of flowers. And E.C., with a pat of putty to cover the grievous wound in his

101

forehead, looking not at all like his natural self, with powdered face and ruby red lips, with his hair combed all wrong, did not speak nor tell her of his misfortune.

The widow does not understand how anyone could do this to E.C. — as gentle a man as there ever was — a man who would give the shirt off his back to a stranger. He had so loved being the police.

All night, her E.C. lay alone amid the flowers, where adjoining rooms held other dead. But such company was no company at all to him. And she thought of him there alone, all night, alone.

Would you please tell me the truth, she begs a God she has long trusted, but one who seems not to listen much these days to newly minted widows.

The silence is crushing.

Bonnie awakes feeling strange. Feeling she has been watched. But there is only Clyde in the room there with her. Clyde asleep still, his mouth partly open, his hair mussed, sleeping in his undershirt and trousers, his shoes. Ready for anything, any sort of trouble — a pistol on the pillow next to his face. An automatic rifle there in the corner with morning light creeping up its stock slow and steady as a snake in search of a rodent.

Walking softly into the living room she sees Ray Hamilton on the sofa. Ray, shirtless, curly blond hairs springing from his chest. Sleeping in his underwear, his legs sleek as bone. Socks and shoes. She cannot help but notice his erection.

She does walk past him and into the kitchen to make a pot of coffee, does not see the wet gleam behind his slit eyes following her.

From the little window above the sink she looks out onto the fallow fields, out onto the vast silent land where once great herds of cattle were driven north to Kansas by yipping cowhands: baby-faced boys in broad hats with lariats and twenty-dollar horses.

Oh, she should write more poems about such things and fewer ones about the life of crime. Fewer ones, about death — cheap or otherwise.

The coffee percolates inside the small glass dome, the blue gas flame dances against the scorched metal bottom.

Then he is standing there suddenly as a summer storm. Standing so close she doesn't have to turn around to know it's him. He smells of old sweat and stale cigarettes and hair oil. He smells of lust.

That's right, she'd tell anyone who wanted to know.

You can smell lust on a guy.

Only it's not something you can describe exactly.

He stands there silently, breathing through his nose, offering her something she tells herself she doesn't want.

"What's cooking, good-looking?"

"Don't be cheap," she says and tries to move away.

But he won't let her, not quite.

"You want me to call Clyde?"

"That what you really want to do, call Clyde?"

She turns and his face is right there in front of hers.

"Don't," she says.

"Don't what?" And his hands come to hold her waist, there, just above her slender hips. Holding her like a Kewpie doll he's just won at the carnival.

"Don't do that," she says.

"This?" he says.

"Yeah, that."

And bang, he's kissing her mouth.

Her fear is instant: Clyde could walk in and see them, go crazy and kill them both over something she keeps telling herself she doesn't want. But she does nothing to stop it either because she's seen about all the guys shot she wants to for one week.

Then Ray stops it.

"What?" he says. "Tell me you didn't like that."

"I didn't like that and if you do it again . . ."

"Don't worry," he says, "I won't."

At least he was decent enough to put on a pair of trousers before he came into the kitchen.

He goes out the back door, walks across open field toward the privy.

She watches him from the window.

He doesn't look back until just before he reaches the little outhouse.

She turns away from the window. He was smiling at her.

Later she fixes them all red beans and eggs for breakfast.

Ted Hinton is a little surprised at how much kick a submachine gun has.

"Take your time with it, son," the instructor says. "You don't have to be accurate like you would a forty-five. You just have to aim it in the general direction and hold her steady — let her do all the dirty work."

"Like this?"

"Yeah, like that."

And Ted Hinton thinks to pity the poor bastard who gets in front of one of these as the chatter of metal scorns his ears, as he watches the paper target torn to shreds.

"It's like having sex with a beautiful woman," the instructor says, "ain't it, son?"

Ted Hinton flushes crimson. He has never had sex with a beautiful woman.

"Yes sir, I guess it is."

The man smiles around a cheek full of Red Man Chew.

"It'll plum knock the shit out of anybody who comes at you," the instructor says, taking back the submachine gun. "Old Tommy here will . . ."

That night Ted has a sex dream that ends in a nocturnal emission. . . .

Rat-a-tat-tat — the hot burst of lead, of cum . . .

. . .that leaves him confused, embarrassed, thinking of the girl he let get away who used to serve him pie and coffee. The police barracks is as silent as the dark side of the moon.

Clyde is restless. Clyde is pacing.

"Fuck this."

Bonnie looks up from the magazine she's reading.

Master Detective.

Ray is slouched on the sofa, his right leg crossed over his left, smoking a cigarette, watching her read.

"What's wrong, sugar?" Bonnie says.

"Everything."

"This heat," Ray says. But doesn't say what about the heat.

"You didn't have to shoot those guys last night," Clyde says.

"And what, just let them arrest me?"

"Fuck," Clyde says again.

"Ice cream," Bonnie says. "Why don't we take a drive and get some ice cream."

She sees Ray watching her, remembers the taste of his mouth. Bitter, like rainwater drunk from a ditch.

She sees him rubbing his knuckles, the sinew of his forearms. Dust motes dance in a shaft of light that slices down the center of the room. Clyde wears brown shoes. Ray wears black.

"I could stand something to drink, myself," Ray says in a jittery manner.

"Ice cream, booze! You two act like this is a lark." Clyde is nervous. Clyde is hot. Clyde is irritated.

Bonnie feels a deep ache of something needing release from her body.

She goes to the bedroom and begins a letter to her mother.

Dear Ma,
    Don't believe what you may read in the

paper about Clyde and me. They are saying we've done a lot of things we didn't. I'm not saying we're angels or anything, we're not. But we're not as bad as they are saying in the newspapers and on the radio. I'm okay. Clyde takes good care of me. Clyde loves me. I love him. That's the way it is and that's how it's going to stay. I miss you terribly. I am going to tell Clyde to bring me for a visit. We will have to be discreet. If the law comes around and asks anything, don't tell them anything. They are just trying to get us in more trouble, blame us for every little crime they can't solve. It's easier to blame everything on Bonnie & Clyde than to find out the real culprits . . .

Then suddenly Ray is standing in the doorway, scratching the tiny gold hairs of his chest.

"Where's Clyde?"

"He went for a drive. Said he had to get some air."

"Why don't you do the same."

"Me? Who needs air?"

She starts to come off the bed.

He's there to take hold of her.

"Don't, I said."

"That was before, this is now."

She closes her eyes. His mouth is hungry. His mouth is wet.

"Clyde will kill you," she murmurs.

"He'll kill us both."

"Let me go."

"Not really," Ray says, and moves her back onto the bed.

His body is hard, forceful, his hands quick.

"I'll say you raped me . . ."

"No, you won't."

She slaps his face hard. He touches where the sting is.

"I like that," he says. "Do it again."

She does.

"Goddamn," he says. "You're really something."

"Don't ruin my dress."

He rolls off, rolls on his back, watches her stand, remove her dress.

"You're never going to leave me alone until I give you what you want, are you?"

"You got that right. Besides, I got a notion you want it too."

"You're wrong, mister."

"Sure I am."

And at last Ray sees what he's been wanting to see for a long time and he likes what he sees and tells himself he's going to like it even more. Bonnie's pale thin body is the stuff of dreams. Ray is amazed at how dark around her nipples she is.

"Just this once," she says. "Then you make up an excuse with Clyde why you can't stay, why you have to get gone."

He reaches for her. She does not come.

"I mean it."

"Okay," he says.

"If not, I'll figure out a way to kill you — or get Clyde to kill you."

"Okay."

"You think I'm kidding?"

He looks into her eyes. They are no longer soft, vulnerable eyes.

"No, I don't think you're kidding. I think you'd do it."

And there in the stifling room with the water-stained wallpaper that once was a soft beige with tiny pink roses, Bonnie gives herself to another man she does not love. Pretending she is doing this act for Clyde, to protect him from something more dangerous later on. She tries not to think of her mother, or the platinum dream she once had of becoming an actress, a poet, someone famous, even as Ray utters:

"Oh, oh . . ."

Even as she hopes her body will not respond to him — but it eventually does.

10

Stolen Kisses

She listens from the open door as she hears Ray explain to Clyde he wants to go home to visit his father. Clyde questions why the sudden change of heart. Clyde cajoles, saying how the next score will be a big one and they can all go home for a visit. Clyde seems in despair. Bonnie is already making plans for how she will kill Ray if he doesn't go, how she will get Clyde to kill him. What sort of wild story can she make up. She doesn't know.

"Okay," she hears Clyde finally say. "Okay, you want to go see your old man, I'll take you myself."

"No," Ray says. "Michigan is a long way. Best we not get caught together. This is the best thing maybe, the three of us breaking up. That's what the law is looking for — two guys and a woman. Me alone would be safer."

"There's not much in the way of dough I

111

can give you," Clyde says. "Unless you want we should knock off someplace first."

"No, I got a little. I got enough for a train ticket."

Then there is the silence between two men unsure what more to say to each other and Bonnie feels great relief when at last they drop Ray off in front of the train station in Dallas, a risky move to be sure — being back in Dallas. But it is near midnight and the streets are fairly empty. And for one brief moment Ray's eyes meet hers as he stands under a streetlight looking into the car's open window.

Then he says, "You take care — both of you."

Driving away she asks Clyde if she can stop and visit her mother.

"You'll cry a river if I don't, won't you?" he says.

"You know how much I love her."

"Sure, I know. You love her as much as me?"

"I love you the same, only different."

"You do, huh?"

The question sounds strange coming from him.

That afternoon when he came back to the house he didn't act like he was suspicious of anything. She was nervous. Ray was

112

taking a nap on the sofa. Clyde carried in a sack of groceries.

"What'd you two do while I was gone?" is all he said, but not in a suspicious way or anything. She told him she'd written a letter to her mother. Had written some poems. He asked her to read him one. She hadn't written any poems. There hadn't been any time. And after, she felt a little sick to her stomach with regret at her betrayal. She got a bad headache.

Ray had thanked her and gone out and smoked a cigarette and then went to sleep on the sofa.

So she found a poem in her notebook she'd written sometime back, one she'd never read to Clyde before and read it to him while he put away the groceries. The poem was called "Blame It on Bonnie & Clyde." He grinned when she finished reading it.

"You know, I think I could use a little loving," he said.

She was surprised. She was afraid. What if Clyde . . .

It wasn't very good. She cursed herself for thinking it wasn't as good with Clyde as it had been with Ray. But that part didn't matter, she told herself. All that mattered was she loved Clyde. He needed her, and she needed him. And after, he curled up beside her, his head nuzzled against her neck, his arm encircled around her waist.

"Well, that's it, then," Clyde says as they drive away from the train station. "I'll have to find us some new guys."

"Why do we need anybody?" she asks.

"You need guys if you're ever going to make a big score," he replies. "We can make a lot of little scores, just me doing the work, but never nothing big like a bank."

"I can help you," Bonnie says in a decision she knows is momentous.

"Hey, I don't want you getting hurt or anything," he says.

"I'd rather be dead than go back to jail."

They drive through the empty Dallas streets, Clyde forever vigilant for police cars.

"I don't like the thought of it."

"You don't have to. Let me try and if things don't work out, then you can get some new guys to help you. Something small, something safe."

He rubs his jaw, lights a cigarette, lights her one.

"We'll see."

She wants to do this thing for him, maybe in part to make up for what she did with Ray, to prove her loyalty, to prove how much she truly loves Clyde Barrow, to show him how much she loves him.

The young man is sitting with his heels resting on a brine barrel. It is one of those days when business is slow. Traffic at the crossroads is uncommon, nonexistent. Still he hopes someone will come in, buy something — a loaf of bread, some milk, anything. He needs this job. He is getting married in a month. There could be a child on the way already. Such news was delivered a few nights earlier while parked in his uncle's sedan under a half-moon with his girlfriend whom he isn't crazy in love with, but who gives herself to him easy enough.

"I'm six weeks late," she said.

He was smart enough about things to know what she meant, this future wife of his, the way it looked, if it was true about her being knocked up. You just didn't knock a girl up and not marry her. Thing was, Edith wouldn't have been his first choice for a wife. Edith was on the heavy side. Edith was not that pretty. Edith was a little sloppy. Edith was a lot like Edith's mother who was large and sad most of the time.

The young man wondered why he'd gotten himself into such a pickle.

But such thoughts were put aside at the sound of an automobile stopping outside, the closing of a car door, the ache of weight on the wood steps, the creak of the screen door opening.

Oh, my, he thinks when he sees the petite young woman come into his store — his uncle's store. She was a real looker.

"May I help you, miss?"

"Oh, I need to get some cheese and bologna and some bread, thank you."

"Yes, ma'am." He is more than happy to help her.

He slices the cheese. He slices the bologna.

"How much worth?" he asks.

"About fifty cents is all."

"Yes, ma'am."

"Careful and not cut your finger off," she teases.

"Oh, no, ma'am, I wouldn't ever do that."

"Hard to count to ten, you did," she says.

He laughs. He feels almost giddy. She seems sweet and flirty even.

He realizes he's staring. She doesn't seem to mind. She smiles in a way that makes him wish now more than ever he hadn't gotten Edith knocked up. There are so many good-looking women in this world . . .

And when he finishes slicing the cheese and the bologna and getting a loaf of bread from the shelf and turns back to face her again is when he sees the gun in beauty's hand.

"Hey, is this some sort of joke?" he says, the grin still stuck on his face.

"No joke, sonny boy. I want the money too."

And at last Bonnie Parker does understand fully the powerful seduction of holding a loaded gun, of pointing it, of seeing the look on a person's face whom it is pointed at.

"Hurry it up there," she commands, waggling the gun just a bit.

Everything in the young man wilts, the grin included. He prays silently he will live long enough to marry Edith, that he will have beautiful children by her, that he will die very old and in a peaceful way. It does not matter that she might grow fat like her mother.

There is just thirty-four dollars in the cash register.

"Put it in the sack with the food," Bonnie says.

He gladly obeys.

"You were hoping for something better to happen here today, I bet," she says.

"I guess I was."

"Maybe next time it will. Now lie down on the floor and don't get up for ten minutes. I'd hate to shoot a nice young man like yourself."

He is glad to lie there against the warm wood boards, and does not breathe, it seems, until the screen door slaps shut, until he hears the roar of the automobile engine, the sound of gravel flung by racing tires, the dead silence that follows.

Bonnie is excited. Bonnie can't stop talking.

"I can't believe it," she says over and over again.

Clyde wears a wry smile.

"You been bit by the gun bug," he says.

"The what bug?"

"The first time you see what it does, it's like a drug."

"No, it's like sex your first time," she says.

"Yeah, I guess."

"It's really something, Clyde."

"I know it is."

They find a lonely place down a back road. A place where there is a cattle pond with no cattle around it. They take a blanket from the backseat and climb the three strands of barbwire fence that is there to keep the nonexistent cattle from wandering out onto the road, and make a picnic — eating the stolen bologna and cheese and bread. Clyde counts the money.

"Your first real score," he says. "Not exactly like knocking over an armored car or something."

She finishes her sandwich, lays her head in his lap. Clyde never rests, remains vigilant for the law.

"The other day when I was gone," he says after a long silence in which Bonnie knows he has been thinking. "What'd you and Ray do?"

Her heart skips a beat.

"I thought I told you, I wrote my mother a letter, wrote a poem. I even read it to you."

"You read me that poem a long time ago."

She sits up, looks into his eyes.

"You think I'd do something with Ray? You think I'd cheat on you with Ray?"

"He told me you did."

It is like a punch in the chest.

"He's lying. He's a goddamn son of a bitching liar."

Clyde looks sad. Clyde looks hurt.

"I know I'm not the greatest lover . . ." he begins to say.

"You're enough for me."

"I mean I can understand how you'd be attracted to other guys. I know they sure are attracted to you. But if you . . ."

She puts her fingers to his lips.

"He's a liar."

"Okay, maybe so."

She kisses him. He doesn't kiss her back. She kisses him again, and this time he does kiss her back, but tentative like a schoolboy his first time kissing.

"Ray Hamilton is a liar, Clyde. And if you don't believe me, you can just take me back to my mother's and drop me off and never see me again."

In the distance they hear a train's whistle.

In the distance they hear birds chirping.

In the distance they hear their hearts beating.

"I will never leave you, Clyde. And you will never leave me. Till death do us part, isn't that what they say when you marry someone?"

"You're the expert," he says, "you're already married."

"Real marriage is a thing of the heart, not something written on a piece of paper. I'm married to you, and till death do us part."

She strokes his hair. He touches her cheek. There is a knowledge shared between them — one that is mysterious and deep as ancient rivers, one from whose water only they can drink.

"I want to kiss your skin," he says.

She removes her dress, her underwear.

"Kiss me," she says. "Kiss me everywhere, Clyde."

She lies back, feels the sun hot against her flesh, feels Clyde's tender nibbling mouth.

"That's it," she says. "That's it."

There on the blanket beside the lovers are the remains of stolen food, and thirty-four dollars weighted under a stone.

11

Enchanted Hearts

Thirty-four dollars does not stretch long: a tourist cabin for a couple of nights, gasoline, meals. It goes like that.

"We got to take something down," Clyde says.

"Like what, honey?"

"Like a bank, I'm thinking."

"A bank? I thought you said you needed some guys for that."

"I don't have any guys, in case you haven't noticed."

Clyde's mood is as foul as the weather.

The skies boil with gray clouds, with gloom and thunder.

Roads are slick from dust turned to slime from hard rain.

Cattle standing out in the fields look forlorn.

Houses seem hunkered down.

Nobody moving. Nobody working.

It is like that across the futile land —

gloom and doom — bankers leaping from the tenth story to go splat against pavement, once-proud men standing in lines for a bowl of soup, women with their hopes crushed inside their defunct dreams. Only the children seem oblivious to it all. Only the children continue to laugh and sing.

Oh, the Missouri countryside looks dully green and blotted damp under the ill weather.

Bonnie watches the window of the V-8 weep raindrops while betrayal buzzes in her brain like a fat bee seeking to sting the flower of her heart.

And Clyde aches to rob something.

Into a small lonely little town they do drift.

Cruising the streets until Clyde does see a lonely little bank, as if it is waiting just for him, its stony edifice darkly wet, its brass plaque a green patina, like the jaded eyes of old love.

Clyde pulls over to the curb. Does not cut the motor.

"This is it," says he.

"Are you sure, honey?"

"Sure as I'll ever be. Why this is a pushover. Stay-tuned, kiddo, we'll be back on top." Bonnie wonders when they ever were on top as Clyde takes out his pistol. Even the pistol is stolen. Such is the criminal's lament. Into the bank he saunters only to come out again in less than a minute, his brow furrowed, his mouth a grim slash, and does drive off in a hurry.

"What happened?" Bonnie is quick to ask, even as the V-8 is careening 'round corners and on out of town again.

"You know what the son of a bitch said?"

"Who, honey?"

"The guy inside the bank."

"What did he say?"

"He said the bank went out of business three months ago. So I says, 'Well, if it's gone out of business what are you still doing here?' and he says, 'I got no place else to go, mister. This job is all I ever had.' Can you believe it? Of all the fucking bad luck!"

And soon the sedan is fishtailing down muddy back roads of the dreary Missouri kind and it looks like more bologna and cheese sandwiches for supper tonight.

And when darkness descends again, with rain drumming on the roof of the auto, Bonnie confesses she has an aunt living in New Mexico who might just enjoy a visit, and that perhaps they should go there for a little while until the law cools off.

Clyde chews silently his sandwich and thinks how it is a lot like living under the Houston Street viaduct, being on the run, eating and sleeping in the car.

"Life feels like it just keeps repeating itself," he says. "Like a bad dream you keep having over and over and can't wake up from."

Bonnie touches his wrist in an understanding way.

"I wish I had Buck with me," Clyde laments.

"Who's Buck?"

"Why I told you about my brother."

"No, honey, you have not."

And so for a little while they talk about Brother Buck, who is currently serving time in Huntsville ("Same place as me"), and how he is due to get out soon.

Clyde shows Bonnie a photograph of the two of them he keeps in his wallet.

It's an old photograph with ragged edges, a cracked seam from having once been folded. Buck is the larger of the two, older-looking. They look like any other pair of poor kids, rough and ready for anything, arms around each other's shoulders, smirks on their faces, dark-haired and handsome with futures undetermined.

The rain increases to a staccato. The sound makes Bonnie sleepy.

Clyde smokes a cigarette, the bright, burning tip floating inside the darkened interior like a restless eye.

Bonnie rests her head on Clyde's shoulder, sighs, "Ummm," and falls asleep.

Clyde listens to the rain, hating what he has become.

His little Bonnie asleep beside him.

Two days' time finds them in New Mexico.

"You know what they call it?" Bonnie says as black mesas loom, as the earth turns powdery red, as canyons lay hidden. "The land of enchantment."

"Why?" Clyde asks.

"I don't know."

"Billy the Kid used to run wild around here somewheres."

"No kidding."

They pass a motor court with cement teepees.

"Look at that," Bonnie says.

"Yeah, whoever heard of Indians living in cement teepees?"

They laugh. Maybe New Mexico ain't such a bad idea, Clyde thinks, wondering how fat the banks are in the Land of Enchantment

126

and are the cops straight shooters? Clyde Barrow, Billy the Kid — has a ring to it, doesn't it? Maybe a hundred years from now they'll be talking about me like they still talk about Billy; the rumination is a pleasant one.

And eventually they do pull up in the yard of Aunt Nettie's house, which is small and white under the nearly flawless turquoise sky. The little aging woman proves to be warm and gracious, small and thin as a half-starved Indian with eyes black as a skillet bottom.

"Lord be," Aunt Nettie says at the sight of Bonnie Parker and hugs her like a lost child found before casting a glance at Clyde Barrow. "And who is this handsome young man?"

After it is all explained — the lie being that they are on their honeymoon, on their way to California, where Bonnie plans to go into acting in the movies — and a nice supper of fried chicken, okra, red beans, and iced tea is consumed, everyone settles in to listen to the radio. To listen to Walter Winchell until drowse overtakes them.

"Isn't it all so nice here?" Bonnie asks, shedding her dress in sleepy fashion there in an attic room before sliding nude into bed next to Clyde.

"Sure, it's swell. Swell as can be."

"Oh, Clyde, don't be such a grump."

"Who, me?"

She can't tell if he's teasing or not; she's too tired to care.

"Well," Aunt Nettie explains the next morning over a breakfast of thick-cut bacon, scrambled eggs, powder milk biscuits, and coffee — "yes, we do have rattlesnakes out here, Clyde."

Clyde woke with a thought in the middle of the night. Bonnie lying facedown snoring softly. I could use some target practice and shooting snakes would be just the thing.

Clyde does explain how big and many are the rattlesnakes in Texas and Aunt Nettie says in reply, "Oh, I'd never fool with them myself. They scare me to death."

Later that morning while washing dishes together, dear aunty asks what is all that noise she is hearing in the not too distance, to which the coquettish Bonnie says, "That is Clyde shooting snakes."

"My Lord, what's he shooting them with?"

"Why it sounds like he is shooting them with his rifle."

The burr of the Browning Automatic

Rifle carries across the undulating land, bounces off canyon walls and mesas in a ricocheting tumult that alarms the old girl's fragile heart.

"Oh, dear!"

"Clyde's just wild about guns," Bonnie says.

Later Clyde returns, deposits the big rifle in the backseat of the Ford, and enters the house.

"Well?" Bonnie says expectantly.

Clyde scratches the back of his head.

"A cup of coffee sounds good to me," he says.

Aunty explains that every day she takes a siesta, right after lunch. They all agree it sounds like a terrific idea. It is during this somnolent moment there is a knock at the door. Clyde is instantly alert. Bonnie is instantly alert. Only dear aunty seems oblivious, dreaming as she does of a beau she had while still a young beauty — a young man who wore his hair parted down the middle and was a gallant soldier in the First World War.

Bonnie and Clyde know the routine of what to do when strangers knock at doors.

And when Bonnie answers the knock

(while Clyde scurries out the back, pistol in each hand), she sees before her a tall, handsome stranger looking as though he rode right straight off the silver screen. For he is standing under a broad-brimmed hat the color of a dove and sweat-stained. He is wearing a shirt with pearl buttons. He has strapped on his hip a six-shooter with horn grips slid down in a hand-tooled holster. He is standing in cowboy boots!

"Howdy, miss."

She nearly swoons.

He explains who he is. The Law.

Too late, too late, Clyde is behind him now, saying throw up your hands, things like that.

Just like the movies it seems, only this isn't the movies, and the spell cast by the handsome stranger is broken by Clyde's tough talk.

Aunt Nettie appears behind her lovely young niece.

"What in the world?"

And is told there is no time to explain, and thank you kindly for the hospitality, but me and Clyde must go.

The old girl watches, her heart thumping like the hind legs of a caught rabbit, as Clyde shoves the deputy into the backseat handcuffed and hopeless, his fate uncertain.

Watches, she does, until the black automobile has disappeared amid the red dust and beyond the broken horizon.

"If you're going to shoot me, I'd just as soon you do it now and not too far away," the lawman says calmly.

"Why?" Clyde asks, pointing his gun at the lawman's heart as Bonnie drives full bore.

"I'd just not like to die too far from home is all the reason I can give you."

"I guess it's a good enough reason," Clyde says.

And hours later when they all see the TEXAS STATE LINE sign loom and then fade in the distance again, the lawman thinks: *Of all the goddamn places to die, Texas would have to be the worst.*

Clyde's a talker, the lawman thinks. Never shuts up. Nervous, twitchy fellow. The kind that would shoot you without thinking twice. But I've gone up against worse. It's the quiet ones that scare me most. If this punk would give me half a chance, it wouldn't be no contest. But then . . . Oh, there is that fear not for self, but for others — the dreaded thought of wife and children spending lonely days, of too little money for them if he were to die like this, so foolishly in Texas . . .

And there at that dusting hour when sun fades low and spreads itself across the very face of the land, the motor stops, doors open.

"Get out," Clyde orders. The lawman is well prepared for this final act, has made as much peace with God in as contrite silent prayers as he knows how. *I should have worn out my knees in church more than I did,* he ruminates. But does assume God is forgiving of sinners and lawmen who chew and smoke and have shot a few fellows along the way.

"Have a good day, sir," Clyde says, and waves before getting back into the Ford behind the steering wheel. And the young woman does also wave as well, her smile pretty there in the evening light, her hair catching fire with the last rays of that beautiful blaze of sun.

"Make sure you tell them Bonnie and Clyde aren't as cold-blooded as everyone says," Bonnie shouts as Clyde drives away, for once in no great hurry.

"I do believe that fellow was surprised I didn't shoot him, don't you?" Clyde says.

"I think he was happy," Bonnie says.

"He should be."

"I'm happy too."

"Why's that?"

"Because we didn't have to hurt him."

"He's lucky, I guess."

Bonnie looks back, sees the lone figure growing smaller, darker, until he becomes a speck, knowing he knows he will return home again to hearty embraces, even though later they hear on the radio that it has been announced this man was murdered by

Bonnie & Clyde,
The Deadly Duo,
The Gun-Toting
Romeo & Juliet.

Oh, Texas and all points everywhere, beware. Beware!

12

Love in the Time of Winter

Bonnie grows homesick. Clyde does too.

"We are alone, truly," she says.

"I know it," says Clyde.

The air has turned cold as iron. Summer's gone. Autumn's come and gone. The last rusty leaves have fallen. Trees stand bare black, like charred skeletons. The daunting winter seems to steal their hearts. Nags them. Leaves them bored and restless as all get out.

"My fingers get so cold I can't hardly hold my gun," Clyde says there in the dark, the windows of the Ford frosted over. Wrapped in a blanket, coats, gloves, they shiver.

"I don't even feel like writing," Bonnie says.

Clyde smokes, thinking it will warm him on the inside.

Earlier they ate soup from cans cooked over an open fire that the wind worried and tried its damnedest to snuff.

"This ain't no kind of life, is it?" Clyde says.

"It's about all the life we got, honey."

Bonnie tries her best to stay upbeat. But lately she's been having bad dreams.

"If it were just me, I wouldn't care so much," Clyde confesses. "But I got you to worry about."

"You don't have to worry about me." Bonnie's teeth chatter.

"Sure I do. That's all I do is worry about you. I sure got you in some mess, huh?"

"No, you didn't get me in any mess I didn't want to be in. Just hold me and keep me warm, okay."

They sit silent for a time, holding each other within the wool blanket. It's like the cold has teeth and is eating them. Gnawing right through the floorboards and through the metal and through the glass just to eat them alive.

Snow begins to fall silently from a bruised sky.

"I can't even imagine how them people way back a hundred years ago stood it," Clyde says. Bonnie's thin body trembles.

"Say, I got an idea. Why don't we go home for a visit? A Christmas visit."

Clyde is suddenly alert, animated, the

cheer back in his voice.

The thought of warmth, of home-cooked food, of a comfortable bed to sleep in, of seeing her mother again fills Bonnie with overwhelming joy, causes her to weep.

"Aw, don't be getting gushy on me, now," Clyde says, but happy in his own heart he'll see family again, his mother and sister, and maybe even Buck if he's out of the pen. Boy, it sure would be good to see Buck again. Buck's the one guy he can really trust. The only person he can trust completely aside from Bonnie.

Bonnie reaches for him there under the blanket. Strokes him to arousal. He wonders if he should protest. It's so goddamn cold he'd hate for anything to freeze and fall off.

"Maybe we should celebrate a little, huh?" Bonnie says coquettishly.

Bonnie is persistent when her needs are upon her and so Clyde does not protest or try to move her hand away. She would see it as a rebuff and pout for days. Instead he allows the long, slow crawling ache to tremble through his blood, to set him ablaze and break his bones.

"I love you so much, Clyde Barrow. I love you so much . . ."

And with snow falling he closes his eyes and keeps them closed until the deed is complete, until he hears the gurgle in Bonnie's throat, knowing that it is not just him alone she is pleasuring, but herself as well. He is simply the instrument of her pleasure, a thing to behold on a winter's night, a distraction to ward off the empty chill that has long invaded them both.

And out there beyond the falling snow and darkness awaits familial love and familiar faces with known histories. And the law will just have to wait its turn.

On this same winter's night, Ted Hinton does sit alone in a stark-lit café drinking coffee, a half-eaten slice of cherry pie on his plate; his taste for pie all but gone these days. For he has been reading of the exploits of one Clyde Barrow and one Bonnie Parker — the "Lawless Lothario and His Cigar-Smoking Moll" as they have recently been dubbed in one local newspaper.

Oh, there was even a little cartoon of the pair of them, armed to the teeth, this duo of growing infamy, guns blazing. He could hardly bear it, the thought of Bonnie like that, consorting with such a man, doing such things as she was accused of. But worse, was the perceived intimacy the two of them must certainly share.

The tales he's read of banks robbed, of

filling stations robbed, of grocery stores robbed, of men shot, of lawmen shot, well, they've just lain heavy as hell on his heart ever since, that's for sure.

He remembers Bonnie, elbows on a gleaming countertop, her chin cupped in her hands, smiling at him, saying, "Hey, how you been lately, Ted?" even though she'd see him every day. He remembers the red bow of her mouth, her pretty small teeth when she smiled, her slender little body. What could a girl like that possibly see in a gangster?

In his lament he does notice that it has begun to snow and thinks of the long lonely walk back to his apartment. And the walk is just as he imagines it: cold and joyless. And the apartment is just as he imagines it — dark and pitiless and without the warmth of a woman.

Turns on a single light. Sits there on the sofa.

Tomorrow it will be Christmas.

It doesn't feel like Christmas.

It doesn't feel like much.

W. D. Jones is instantly smitten with Clyde. A kid whose folks did take up residence under the same Houston Street viaduct in those hard days of Clyde's youth, of whom

Clyde did play a little catch with out of mostly boredom tossing to and fro an old rag baseball — W.D. a good six or seven years younger.

Oh, it is a meager celebration as celebrations go. The gifts are few and mostly cheap, the gin made in a bathtub, the cigarettes hand-rolled.

Family fawns over Clyde, frets inwardly at what a mess the boy has gotten himself into. But Buck is there with his new wife — Blanche — a dark-haired beauty who clings to him and does not drink bathtub gin or anything with the "spirits to them."

"Where's Bonnie?"

"She's visiting her mother."

"Oh, we'd love to have seen her."

"You will before we leave again."

The talk of leaving again puts a pall in the not so gay air.

No one wishes to offend Clyde, the darling boy with wild ways, and so no one talks of crime or being chased by the "laws" as Clyde likes to call them. And no one talks of eventualities, for like death it is kept at bay. And death they all know is likely and certain to come sooner than it has a right to in Clyde's case. No one talks of such things except W. D. Jones who seems at first shy but warms up after one or two gins.

His adoration is obvious.

"I don't guess you'd need you a wheelman or a partner, would you?"

"How old are you?" Clyde asks.

"Sixteen now, be seventeen soon enough."

"Wheelman, huh?"

"I'm pretty good with a car."

"You pretty good with a gun, too?"

"Gun? I reckon I could be if I needed to be."

He is a handsome boy, Clyde does think. Reminds Clyde of someone. Oh, yeah. That kid in prison got his throat slit.

Clyde says, "You're too young for such wild pursuits."

"No I ain't."

The kid follows Clyde around like a puppy.

Blanche says, "Glad to meet cha."

"She's a tall drink of water," Clyde tells Buck who grins and grins.

"Ain't she though."

They laugh and swig the bathtub gin and squinch their faces.

Buck plays the ukulele. Sis sings. And soon Mother is playing the piano.

Across Dallas town, Emma Parker does weep with gladness to see her Bonnie again. A Christmas tree smaller than a child stands in the corner of the living room with a single strand of colored lights — red and blue and green — draped 'round its paucity of needled limbs. A few wrapped presents rest on a sheet made to look like snow beneath the tiny tannenbaum.

Bonnie's eyes are full of tears.

"I didn't get you anything for Christmas," she stutters.

"Oh, you're all I ever need. You're the greatest little gift I could ever hope for."

Bawling like babies they cling to each other.

Emma is afraid to ask after the fate of Clyde for fear Bonnie will say they are still in love, forever, and she will have to eventually watch her darling child leave again knowing that each time could be the last time she ever sees her.

They drink eggnog with just a little whiskey in it.

"I don't usually," Mother Emma says. "But it being Christmas and all . . ."

And later gives Bonnie her present — a pair of red gloves that only brings more tears.

They sit up half the night talking.

Till the conversation turns to Clyde and

Bonnie's criminal exploits.

"Tell me you never shot anyone or hurt anyone," her mother pleads.

"I never did . . .and Clyde never did either. All those things they're saying about us are lies, Mother."

But Emma has it no longer in her heart to unconditionally believe her own child.

"Bonnie . . ." she starts to say, but Bonnie is intuitive enough to know where the conversation is headed and cuts it short.

"We're not killers and we never will be."

"Oh, God . . ."

And later in the dark, lying on the sofa, Bonnie likes to look at the colored lights of the little tree and hums softly such seasonal hymns as she remembers, hymns about babies born in mangers and wise men and kings and silent nights.

And Mother Emma prays to an unseen God to save her pretty daughter from terrible fates and misdeeds.

"If you must take her from me, don't let it be at the hands of violent men," she offers in a voice as soft as a Christmas hymn.

Clyde and Buck do hold private counsel.

"I could use you, brother," Clyde implores.

"Blanche is a straight shooter, old son."

Clyde explains the economic conditions of the land. Buck nods in agreement.

"Fellows like us can't even find dishwashing jobs," Clyde cites. "And how you going to keep that pretty wife of yours clothed and fed, even on a dishwashing job, which you can't get even if you wanted to?"

Buck looks 'round, sees his lovely Blanche watching the two of them.

"Look here, I wouldn't be in it for the long haul was I to go with you, Clyde."

"I ain't either. Just one big score is all we need. Then we can hightail it down to Mexico or up to Canada or someplace they can't lay a glove on us."

"You're pretty good at this, huh? This robbing banks?"

"I got lot a practice lately."

"I'd have to talk Blanche into going along."

Clyde winks.

"Here's pearls in your oysters."

And as Buck wanders off to explain it to Blanche, W.D. appears and says, "Well, you thought about it — me going with you?"

"Yeah, kid, I thought about it," and drapes his arm around the young man's shoulders.

★ ★ ★

With prayers complete, Mother Emma
does hear from the living room the sweet
twining voice of her daughter singing "O
Little Town of Bethlehem" and cannot
imagine such a voice being forever silent.

"Death, if you need someone, take me," she
mutters through the haze of whiskey-laced
eggnog.

13

The Love Dreams of Bandits

Well, Mama, here we are in Joplin. Just the five of us: Clyde and me, Buck and Blanche, and a handsome young man named W. D. Jones. I don't think you know him. He's a friend of Clyde's and just a kid really. We have been traveling a lot, been to Oklahoma twice, all over Missouri as well. I don't like Missouri much, but it is safe from the laws. Blanche has a little white dog we all just love. Buck says she loves that dog more than him. Blanche is okay in my book, but it is hard living with a lot of other folks all in one house. W. D. idolizes Clyde. I think he'd do anything for him. He's cute. Did I mention that? Hope you are well and I hope I get to see you soon. I've been putting the bug in Clyde's ear to bring me for a visit. He says he will soon as it's safe. Don't worry about me, I'm doing swell.

All my love, Bonnie.

Clyde's still yammering about the botched stolen car job where a man was shot. W. D. got rattled, flooded the man's automobile. The man ran out, jumped on the running board — big man, angry as hell. Grabbed Clyde by the knot of his tie.

"Hey, this is my brand-new sedan!" he shouted. Clyde got the motor started, took off down the street, the man holding on to Clyde's necktie. "Choking me to damn death!" Clyde tells the story for the hundredth time it seems. W. D. sits and listens with his hands pressed between his knees, ashamed. Sits next to Blanche with all the color gone out of her cheeks as she listens to Clyde's tirade.

Clyde paces, strikes the air with his fists.

Brother Buck tries to calm him down.

"Goddamn, old son, things go wrong sometimes."

"They ain't supposed to! But it seems they always do because I hook up with lousy amateurs who say they can do this and that when they can't."

Clyde glares, grits his teeth, stammers, and spits out the words.

Bonnie has heard it all before, knows how explosive Clyde's temper can be.

She writes of such tirades in her *journal* — another new Big Chief tablet she's recently

146

purchased at a Five & Dime to replace the one left at the apartment. She copies into it as well, from memory, her old poems, and begins new ones. She writes what leaps from her brain, flames of incidents and feelings.

"He's just sixteen," she says to Clyde, which momentarily seems to stem the tide of his anger.

"Hell, old son," Buck chimes in. "When we was W.D.'s age, we were just as green."

"Maybe you, not me." Clyde has to get the last say in.

On calmer days, Bonnie takes pictures of them all with her box camera, has W.D. take some of her and Clyde together, kissing, holding guns on each other, leaning against the grill of their latest ride.

Now and then she wonders what Ray Hamilton is doing . . . not that she really cares, she tells herself.

But Clyde brings up Ray Hamilton's name quite a lot, tells Buck stories about the two of them, how Ray was a lot cagier guy than he looked.

"He's got this innocent face — like some farmer or something, a face you would trust if you didn't know him better," Clyde says. "But the guy would shoot you in a heartbeat. I seen him do it."

Clyde tells such stories in front of

Blanche: stories of shootings and robberies and life on the run.

Buck says, "Listen, old son, can that sort of talk in front of Blanche, huh? Blanche is here just because I am. She's no moll. She's not like Bonnie."

Night after night, Bonnie and Clyde can hear Blanche and Buck going at it in the next room. The walls are thin as sliced cheese. The beds are cheap. Blanche is no shrinking flower when it comes to expressions of her pleasure. Neither is Buck.

Clyde says more than once: "That kind of thing is embarrassing to listen to."

Bonnie waits for her lover to take heed, to take heart, to be duly inspired. But Clyde hardly ever does. And when she tries to prompt him, he says, "I don't want everybody in the world to know my private business."

"Well, it's not everybody in the world, Clyde," she counters. "It's just us, and them. They don't seem to mind, why should we?"

"There's that kid out in the other room, too."

"You don't think W.D. knows about such things?"

"I don't care does he know or not, I just care he doesn't know about *my* personal business, is all."

And from bed to window she sometimes paces in sexual heat, in unrequited desire, does look to the moon and stars so lonely and distant. And the winsome young woman does try to ignore the randy ranting of one Blanche and Buck Barrow so as to keep her own desire at the same distance from herself as are the moon and stars.

Over next morning's breakfast, W. D. Jones casts shy glances between the four of them. And once, while Clyde and Buck are in the garage doing something or other — loading guns, checking motor oil levels, and Blanche was indisposed in the small bathroom — Bonnie boldly asks the dark-haired youth if he ever made love to a woman.

He swallows hard, says, "I did to a girl once."

"But have you ever with a woman?"

Sounds coming from the garage, footsteps drawing near, voices growing louder, absolve him of the need to answer.

Bonnie does reply quickly:

"Oh, you don't have to say anything to anyone about this little conversation. I mean it's just between the two of us, understand?"

Clyde and Buck enter the room, their hands greasy, Buck saying, "Where's Blanche?"

For several nights after, sleeping there on the sofa, his feet hanging over the edge, listening to muted passions of Buck, W. D. Jones did lay in a state of confused excitement thinking about the odd way Bonnie had questioned him about his romantic history. He hadn't ever really made love to anyone. The lie he fed Bonnie meant to tarnish his innocence. He would like to dance with her, to hold her the way Clyde did in those photographs he took of the two of them. He would like to kiss her the way Clyde did and have her kiss him that way too. He could not sleep. Sleep would not come until he did something to make it come.

Journal entry: April 18, 1933. Disaster befalls us. The laws were outside waiting on us when Clyde spotted them. They covered the front yard like cockroaches. Somebody shot first, then somebody else. A bullet almost blew off my head, left window glass in my hair. Blanche went crazy, ran out into the street. How she failed getting shot to pieces is a miracle. The boys shot their way out — me with them. How we made it without all being killed, I don't know. W.D. got nicked in the head.

Found Blanche running down the street, that damn little dog in her arms. Buck grabbed her. Had to slap her to get her to stop screaming. We drove like crazy. Bullet holes in the car, back window shot out, headlight blown off. All that shooting made me deaf for two days. Left a pot of beans cooking on the stove, cornbread in the oven. Blanche left her purse, Buck his shoes. Hope those laws enjoyed our dinner. B. Parker.

Ted Hinton feels crisp in his starched shirt — armed and ready for bear. Being the police gives a man the sense of himself. His pistol rides high on his hip like the old-timers showed him to wear it. His boss, Bob, gives him a piece of just-arrived news. A telegram from Joplin, Missouri.

"We're going up there," Bob announces. "Bonnie and Clyde just shot their way out of a fight — killed two peace officers, wounded some others. Local law wants us to go and confirm it's them since they all come from here. Help catch them if we can. You know Bonnie pretty well, don't you, Ted?"

Ted looks at the yellow piece of paper, looks at the names on it.

Lord God. They really did it this time.

Nothing I can do to save her now.

It's one long drive from Dallas to Joplin. Driving through the night is like driving through ink. Headlights bounce along ahead of them. Bob doesn't say much. Bob's not a big talker. He's like most of the police Ted knows: quiet, steady, always thinking about ways to finish a case.

One question keeps haunting Ted's questioning heart:

Would I shoot her if I had to?

Wind sweeps the evening air.

"Where are we?" Bonnie asks.

"Amarillo," Clyde says.

Buck and Blanche and W. D. Jones are all crammed together in the backseat, trying as they might to sleep. But sleep is elusive. W.D.'s head throbs from where the bullet nicked him. Somebody's hand rests on his crotch. He can't see in the dark who the hand belongs to. Buck or Blanche.

A motor court looms on the edge of the dusty town.

Each of them is stung by the wind as they get out and stretch their legs waiting for Blanche to rent them rooms.

"Place smells like cow shit," Buck says wearily.

Clyde remembers the feedlots they

passed — the million or so cattle milling about in each.

Blanche is still a little shocked at waking to find her hand resting on the boy when Clyde cuts the motor. And even though she did quickly recoil, she did not want the boy to think . . .

Gray, knobby fingers of clouds stretched long through a pink dawn sky. A gunman's sky, Bonnie would later call it in a poem, as they yawn and stretch waiting for the less known Blanche to negotiate two rooms with the desk clerk inside the little office.

Clyde has parked the car so that the license plates cannot be easily read. He will send the boy to steal a few more. Clyde likes to keep plenty of spares on hand and change them often. Clyde is a planner. Clyde is learning to be wary.

The deskman lets his bleary eyes rest upon the lovely woman. He has the same hungry look as a man half his age. And when he speaks, his breath comes out sour as milk gone bad. And Blanche is reminded, as she fills out the forms and pays him ten dollars for two rooms, that lust never abandons the mind of men until death comes and snatches them up.

"There's five of you," the man says questioningly as he looks beyond her to the lot of them standing out by the sedan.

"The boy will be sleeping in the car."

"Oh, I see."

"I bet you do."

He looks at her again, the sassy way she says I bet you do, and it stirs up some old memories in him of another time when he was young, wild, a drinking and dancing man.

He watches the sway of her wide firm hips as she walks out and joins the others and thinks of the way it was once down Nuevo Laredo, thinks of good tequila and guitar music and the warm brown flesh of pretty whores.

Bandits, he thinks. *I been around long enough to know bandits when I see them*, then goes back to bed.

And the pink sky dissolves to one of airy blue.

As bandits sleep in their beds.

As old men and boys dream of lovely encounters.

On both sides of the border.

14

Love's Sanctuary

When you were in the pen," Buck says one particular evening while he and Clyde and the kid, W.D., are planning a robbery, "did they ever . . ."

"No!" Clyde says, looking from his brother to W.D. with a glare of caution.

"Did they what?" asks W.D.

"Nothing, kid, forget about it."

Later, alone, Clyde says to Buck, "Why'd you have to bring that up in front of the kid?"

Buck looks off toward the green sedan where Bonnie and Blanche are sitting on the running boards smoking cigarettes, gabbing about who knows what — where W. D. Jones is now squatting on his heels by the grill dangling a pistol from his finger.

"They did me," Buck says.

"They did you what?"

"They did me hard and they did me bad

and I didn't have any say in it because there were too many of them and I got tired of being beat up over it."

"Well, they didn't me," Clyde says, cupping his hand around a struck match he's trying to keep the wind from as he dips his head down to it to light his cigarette.

"I don't see how you could have not . . ."

"Shut up about this stuff. What the hell you want to talk about this stuff for anyway?"

Buck shrugs. Buck stands there with the wind whipping his hair. Buck keeps his fists deep inside his pockets.

"Just that sometimes I see a good-looking kid like W.D. and . . ."

"Shut up, will you."

Clyde lights his cigarette, then lets the wind have its way with the lit match before flicking it away.

"You're a happily married guy," Clyde says without looking at Buck.

"Sure I am."

"Which means you like women, plain and simple. Just like I love Bonnie. There's nothing wrong with us. I mean it's just plain and simple. What happened in the pen to you don't mean nothing."

"I know it don't."

"Then shut up about it."

"I was just wondering if it ever happened to you. It'd make me feel better if I knew."

"Make you feel better? You're cuckoo. How's knowing something like that going to make you feel better?"

"I mean feel better about me, like it wasn't just me it happened to. Like I'm not the only guy who's come out of there and sometimes think the things I do."

"Shut up! I mean it. It didn't ever happen to me. So just shut up."

The rest of the day, Clyde is quiet. Clyde drives fast — southwest out of Oklahoma.

"We going home, sugar?" Bonnie asks.

But Clyde doesn't say yes or no about going home.

But for a flirtatious moment, the undertaker's new Chevrolet might not have been so easily stolen. The thievery occurred while taking final payment for a funeral performed in early spring. The not-so-young widow wanting to make sure "her Herbert's" debts were all taken care of allowed the mortician — a Stanley Jefferson — to make passes at her and suggest that perhaps dinner out someplace nice would not be out of the question; he being a single man, and allowing that certainly an appropriate amount of time had expired

157

between the late mister's death and now. The widow did not demur. The distraction was enough for the "Barrow Gang" to steal away the mortician's new cream-colored coupe.

Clyde does not stop again except to rob a grocery store. The old man and old woman stand with hands raised while Buck rifles the cash register and W. D. Jones the shelves of food. The indignity of it all is plainly etched on the faces of the unfortunate owners.

"Times ain't tough enough without being held up by a bunch of thieves," the old man mutters loud enough for Clyde to hear.

"Shut the hell up!" Clyde warns, waving his pistol.

"You're Bonnie and Clyde," the old woman says. "I know it from the newspapers."

"Yes we are," Bonnie says obligingly. "You can tell everyone you were robbed by Bonnie and Clyde."

"Humph . . ." the old man snorts. "Like that's something I should be proud of."

"Would you rather tell them you were shot by Bonnie and Clyde?"

Clyde is angry, steps close to the old

man, presses the barrel of his pistol into the old man's stomach, gunmetal touching faded denim.

"No sir, I sure wouldn't."

"No sir, I bet not," Clyde mocks.

Miles down the road Bonnie says, "Why were you so mean to those old folks?"

"I just feel mean is all."

Blanche and Buck and W.D. ride silently in the backseat, crammed together. W.D. can feel Blanche's leg muscles twitching against his thigh. He wishes he could just reach over and touch her.

The wail of a siren comes out of nowhere.

Clyde sees a motorcycle policeman in his rearview mirror closing fast.

Directly ahead of them a storm cloud the size of a mountain boils up from the prairie. In its belly they can see lightning flashing. The sky to the east and west of the storm is streaky with rain.

"Maybe we ought to head in a different direction, honey," Bonnie says. "That could end up a tornado."

Clyde lights a cigarette, steering the wheel momentarily with his knees.

"Hell, it should be interesting," he says, and mashes the accelerator down hard and drives straight into the face of the storm.

Bonnie is at first tense with fear. Then feels Clyde's hand patting her knee.

"We'll just go on, no matter what happens," he says. "Just you and me."

Clyde winks.

"Nobody lives forever, ain't that right?"

Blanche is distraught, screaming her fool head off in the back. But Buck understands Clyde's penchant for danger. It is a Barrow trait. It is like an extra bone in the Barrow boys' bodies.

"Go on into it, old son!" Buck shouts even as the roar of the wind howls down upon them, drowning out even the sound of the siren.

Dark gray air washes over them.

Around them is whipped-up dust and grass. Then a smashing rain lashes against the windows. Hail hammers the hood and roof.

The car becomes more like a wild pony they are trying to ride straight into hell than the stolen coupe of an undertaker.

The storm obliterates road and time and geography.

It is a storm of magnificent magnitude — a king of a storm.

Clyde is determined to smash his way through it or have it smash them all.

The pursuing policeman quails, turns his

motorcycle about, and races toward a peaceful horizon. *If it is Bonnie and Clyde I'm chasing — let the storm have them!*

And though Clyde Barrow does not know the meaning of the word, the thrill of smashing into danger is *erotic*.

And once clear of storm and pursuing police, they do find an abandoned farmhouse — one of hundreds of foreclosed homesteads bankrupt of life and hope — and do take up residence for the time being.

Clyde, still with his blood afire from fighting the storm, does lead Bonnie out to the old barn where the scent of hay lingering in its shadowy places is sweet and strong.

"Take off everything, okay," he says, stripping off his shirt and trousers.

"Here?"

"Yes, now."

And when she is fully naked he kneels before her, wraps his arms 'round her waist, presses her to him. Her rump is small and round and firm in his hands.

"I know I ain't been a good lover to you, Bonnie. But it's not because you're not beautiful or that I don't want you . . ."

"Hush, hush," she says.

He feels her fingers stroking his hair.

"Just I got a lot on my mind most of the time . . ."

"No need for talk now, sugar."

"And God knows, I sure do love you . . ."

He presses his face into what he has come to call her *flower* and it shatters whatever doubt she's ever had about the two of them.

"Oh, sugar . . ." she sighs. He pulls her down.

And though his lovemaking is hasty and unschooled, it matters not this time, anyway. She comes with him. And later he lies beside her like a tired schoolboy done with chores, hay dust sticking to his damp skin, and hers.

"Boy, that storm must have eaten that son of a bitch up," W.D. is telling Buck there on the porch. Buck sitting in a busted chair, W.D. on the top step.

"That copper would have been a fool to ride into that storm," Buck replies, looking over toward the barn where he saw Bonnie and Clyde wander into earlier.

"You think?" W.D. grins.

Blanche is inside with a migraine.

"That undertaker must make some damn good money to be driving a new car like that one there," W.D. says, nodding toward the mud-streaked coupe.

"Why don't you quit talking so much?" Buck says.

"Why don't you?"

In this place, Clyde thinks, *I could stay forever, just as I am, here next to Bonnie.*

Above him the shadows are streaked with light seeping through the rotting cracks of boards, through blown-off shingles. And from where he lies, it is like looking up into heaven. For through the shattered shadows and light, birds fly. Birds like doves. Heaven's doves that coo. And beside him is an angel that may have fallen from that heavenly place.

Oh, we're all but fallen angels, really.

Bonnie's penchant for poetry has rubbed off on him some, for listen to the way he's thinking this stuff now.

I like women, he tells himself, full of disdain of his earlier conversation with Buck. *Buck likes 'em too. Nothing happened to me that would change me being a real man.* And reaches out and touches Bonnie, who under his touch stirs and sighs her satisfaction.

And when the end day comes, I'll go down like a man so everyone will know.

But such respite is temporary, and Clyde

Barrow is already starting to feel restless and the need to move on.

Move on to where, he does not know. *Perhaps to true heaven.*

For this life ain't turning out to be nothing but pure hell.

15

Love's Crazy Circle

Suddenly they are falling.

Well, they were speeding along just fine and a sign not far back said ONE-LANE BRIDGE AHEAD. But when they got there, there wasn't any bridge. There was just a place over a wash where a bridge had been before a flood had swept it away: a small and rickety wood bridge that should have been replaced years ago: a bridge that could not withstand the force of swirling brown floodwater against its dry-rot timber. And so it went on down somewhere, smashed and forever lost, and nobody got around yet to replacing it. Times, after all, were hard and there was not much money to replace old bridges. Locals knew other ways to cross the wash, so why bother with something they could just as easy do without.

It is of a late evening and Clyde is driving fast, as usual, and everyone is talking about where they should go next — the last few jobs having been substantially successful, financially speaking, and it does seem they are on a winning streak.

"And," Blanche is happy to intone, "nobody got shot or nothing."

So spirits are running high when the mortician's coupe seems to float for an odd moment, before it plunges and smashes hard in the rocky dry wash.

The automobile balances on its nose for a full several seconds before falling over on its side like a shot beast.

Clyde crawls clear. Blanche and Buck crawl clear. W. D. Jones, his head rattled from being bumped right on the very spot where his wound was, crawls clear.

They all stand dazed, bewildered.

"Where'd the fuck that bridge go?"

Looking up at the gap.

"We're standing in a goddamn dry river."

"No shit."

Then hear Bonnie's painful cries and see the little lick of flame spark up from the leaking gasoline. The coupe has pinned her under it. The flame slithers toward her like an angry cobra.

The men try to lift the automobile off Bonnie while Blanche beats at the flame with her jacket. No good. Clyde and them beat at it too and finally snuff it but not before it gets in a good lick or two on Bonnie's gashed and bleeding leg.

Oh, how she wails.

Clyde scrambles up the embankment remembering a farmhouse whose lights winked in the faded purple haze of coming night. Runs like a son of a bitch to that house ignoring barking dogs and near breaks down the door with his pounding. A large robust man comes forth and goes back down with him to the wreckage and together the four men lift the coupe enough to pull Clyde's hysterical lover free.

All the while she moans and writhes in pain.

Oh, Lord, what unexpected miseries do befall us.

The robust farmer's wife does what she can with strips of an old but freshly washed sheet and hydrogen peroxide.

"It ain't enough," the farmer's wife says. "She needs a doctor."

Well, what Clyde and the others fail to notice is the farmer catching glimpses of the cache of guns spilled all inside the coupe and it gets him to wondering what sort of people drive around with so many guns wearing suits and neckties and pretty red dresses. It isn't as though he lives so far out in the sticks he has never heard of the crimes committed by a gang called the "Barrows." He has.

"I'll go get a doctor," he volunteers, "and be right back."

It seems nobody is thinking straight but the farmer, not even his wife, who does all she can to bring solace to the pain-ravaged young woman with strawberry blond hair.

It isn't until the farmer is long gone that Clyde does realize it is all a ruse to bring the laws.

Lucky for them the old man chooses to go for help in his truck and not in his DeSoto sedan with two new front tires he more or less wants to baby along for a good spell, tires costing what they do these days.

"Oh, dear. Oh, dear," says the farmer's wife, watching them take the pretty little girl and put her in the family automobile and drive off into the lonesome night.

"Well, Lord be," is all she can manage to cry to the caved-in night. "Lord be!"

They stop long enough to gather up the guns before hitting the back roads, Bonnie's head resting on Blanche's lap, her legs and feet across Buck who feels as though his bones are all crunched together.

He is having second thoughts about the luck of Bonnie and Clyde. W.D., for once, rides up front next to Clyde, the two of them smoking cigarettes, the cool night wind whistling in through the DeSoto's wing vents.

"Lord God!" Bonnie yelps every time the auto bounces over some rut or other. It feels nightmarish to her, this thing that has happened. She frets she could lose her leg, that some man in a white coat could take a saw and saw it right off — saw right through flesh and bone. What would she do then? Who would want her one-legged? She'd seen the look earlier in Clyde's eyes back in the farmer's bedroom. Clyde is squeamish at the sight of the bone-deep gash. Clyde would leave her if she only had one leg.

"Hush, hush," Blanche says.

She looks up into Blanche's face, what she can see of it residing deep in shadows, smells Blanche's perfume.

"Whatever happened to that little dog you had — Buster?"

"I don't know," says Blanche.

"It got away in that shootout in Joplin," Buck says.

"That's right, it got away. Hush now, Bonnie, try and close your eyes, take your mind off it."

"I can't, I can't."

Somewhere in the ensuing hours Clyde finds a smooth road to drive on and the steady hum of those new front tires and the old ones on the rear lull Bonnie into a fit-filled sleep wherein she dreams of her mother and her husband Roy Thornton. Only half the time it is Roy and the other half Roy is Ted Hinton. Wakes, falls back into the drowse, wakes again.

Clyde is carrying her into a cabin.

"Where are we, honey?"

"Platte City," says he, and lays her upon a stiff narrow bed in which she can smell the Swanson soap-washed sheets, feel their cool crispness. "Missouri," Clyde adds.

"I hate Missouri," she says.

"I know you do."

She sees W. D. Jones pacing back and forth, pulling back the window shades, looking out.

"I want you to go get my mama," she tells Clyde. "She'll nurse me back."

Clyde looks anxious, disheveled, his eyes half closed with weariness as he changes her bandages. It hurts. Every little time she is touched, it hurts. Clyde winces as though he is pulling the bandages off his own flesh.

Blanche is sent to buy beer and hamburgers. They eat the hamburgers from greasy wax paper, drink the beer straight from the bottles. A shed with the farmer's stolen automobile parked in it separates the cabins of the two couples.

Clyde gives Buck and W.D. instructions.

"You boys need to go do some robbing while I tend to Bonnie."

They exchange doubtful looks.

"We're low on money and Bonnie's in no shape to travel right now and I'm not leaving her."

The instructions are given outside on the cabin's stoop while Blanche plays nurse, washes Bonnie's naked body, careful to be tender with the burnt, slashed leg. Millers and moths circle madly under a bare yard light above their heads.

"Don't rob nothing close. Don't rob nothing anywhere near Joplin. Don't take any chances. Rob out of the way places — stores and filling stations — stick to the back roads afterward. Come back here in a week, Bonnie should be up to traveling by then."

"What if we get caught?" W.D. asks, one foot resting on the stoop's lower step.

"You do it right, you won't get caught. The cops ain't caught us yet and they're not going to unless you do something stupid. Don't do anything stupid."

Buck says, "Boy, I better rip it up tonight if I'm going to be gone from Blanche for a whole week."

"I guess you better, old son," Clyde says with a wry grin.

W.D. gets Buck's meaning, says, "Shooee, I guess I'll go and take me a leak before I turn in," and wanders off into the shadows.

"That kid's got grit, I'll give him that," Buck says. "He didn't piss his pants back there in Joplin."

"He gave them hell, didn't he?"

"He sure enough did."

"You take charge of things while you're gone," Clyde says.

"Don't worry, I ain't going to get none of us caught."

"Killed, either."

"No, I ain't ready to die yet, are you?"

Clyde shakes his head.

"Not hardly."

"Then we'll take off in the morning, me and him, and see you back here in a week."

Buck starts to go into his own cabin. Clyde calls, "I'm glad I got you with me, old son."

Buck waves, goes on in, waits for Blanche to come over from tending Bonnie. Waits there in the bed, ready to rip it up some, missing her already.

★ ★ ★

Clyde sits alone in the dark, the millers and moths above his head drawn to the hot light — crazy it seems in their natural desire to burn themselves up. He knows how it is, to be drawn to something you can't resist, and thinks if I were a miller or a moth, I'd be right there with them, going 'round and 'round that damn light all crazy.

Bonnie sighs under Blanche's delicate nursing.

16

Love on the Run

When the farmer gets through explaining
what he'd been involved in — the gang of
fancy-dressed men and women, all the guns
inside the wrecked coupe — the county
sheriff's blood is dancing.

"You know what I reckon?" the sheriff
says, putting on his hat.

"That they are the Barrow Gang?"

"That's what I reckon."

"Then you'll need some men to go with
you."

"I surely will."

"Holy Jesus!"

"What?"

"I left Sophie with them."

"I never heard of them killing a woman."

"I got to get on back."

"They're most likely on the run again by
the time we get there."

"I guess you hurry, they won't get very
damn far."

"That's what I aim to do. Ain't no auto-mobile can outrun a telephone call."

But the roads prove empty of nefarious types and no Bonnie and Clyde are found. Nor any stolen DeSoto sedan with two new tires on the front.

"Our luck's holding," Clyde says.

Bonnie is feeling better after nearly a week of constant care. Clyde has proven his ministrations are nearly as tender as those of Blanche, his skills as nurse equal. Clyde even runs the risk of hitchhiking into town for fresh bandages, pain pills, a sack of jelly doughnuts. Blanche buys them the same dinner every night — hamburgers and bottles of Schlitz beer.

It is July and the heat is like a warm damp washcloth over the face. On certain nights they can smell the Platte River — an ancient smell of water forever moving since the beginning of time.

Clyde cleans his guns. Clyde smokes Chesterfields; Bonnie, Camels. Blanche is pretty in the evening light — larger-boned than Bonnie, Clyde does notice, with larger breasts and fuller hips. Clyde re-members Buck saying how he was going to have to rip it up the night before him and W.D. went off on a robbing spree.

Clyde has Blanche walk down to the filling station every day at noon to catch the radio news in case Buck or W.D. is captured.

"I'm not fond of that elderly man who works there," she says in mild protest.

"Why's that?" Clyde asks, swabbing out the barrel of one of the rifles with a shred of oily rag.

"Because he is always commenting on how pretty I look."

"Well, you are pretty," Bonnie says, sitting up in bed with pillows propped under her healing leg.

"It's one thing for you to say it, another for that creepy old man to say it."

"Use your charm on him," Clyde says. "Maybe he'll give you a discount on the beer."

"He's already offered that."

"What'd you tell him?" Bonnie asks with a mischievous smile.

Blanche looks at her disdainfully.

"I told him I was a happily married woman, thank you very much."

"Don't tell him nothing you don't have to about us," Clyde says, satisfied the gun barrel is quite clean.

"Don't worry, I won't. He likes to listen to baseball and I have to ask him to please dial on the news and he wants to know why I'm so interested in the news and I tell him I just am, that's all."

"That's the right way to handle him," Clyde says.

"Yeah, but I don't like it, having to lie to people — even nasty old men like him."

Bonnie says to mollify Blanche's sense of propriety, "Well, honey, all men are like that, even the old ones. Ogling women is just something they never get over. Just overlook it, okay?"

And so life repeats itself for a full week until the boys return late one evening — pulling into the shed between the cabins, pulling down the door after them, the motor hot and ticking as it cools from the long haul.

There is a sense of celebration of sorts, having the boys back and safe again.

Clyde is especially anxious to hear all about their adventures, but Buck is taciturn and W.D. says he has hardly slept in three days and falls down on a pallet there in Bonnie and Clyde's cabin.

"I just need to spend a little time with my wife, first," Buck says with the clutching Blanche. "That okay with you, old son?"

Oh, the night is peaceful and Bonnie sits next to Clyde on the stoop, her arm around him saying, "I think everything is going to work out okay, don't you, honey?"

The full moon seems balanced on the branches of a copse of trees.

"You ever get really scared?" she asks.

"Just when it's like this," Clyde says.

"What do you mean?"

"I never get scared when things are tight, when the laws are all over us and shooting at us or chasing us. But when it's like this, when I have time to think and it's all peaceful like it is now, that's when I get scared sometimes, knowing sooner or later they're probably going to catch us. And when they do catch us, I think about what they're going to do to us . . ."

"I'm just the opposite, honey. Right now, I'm not scared at all. I'm happy."

"Hell, I guess that's the difference between us then."

"If anything, I'm homesick, Clyde."

"Me too, a little."

"I'd like us to have a little house all our own someday. Kids, maybe."

Clyde sits with his arms resting atop his knees, the taste of the cigarette's tobacco slightly bitter.

"Well, if that's what you want, sugar," says he, "we best be making plans to go to Mexico, because the laws around here sure ain't going to let us settle down into no house or nothing else."

"Let's not even think about those dirty laws, honey. Let's just concentrate on that old moon there."

Love cannot pierce wood, nor glass nor steel. But surely bullets can.

And bullets can pierce the heart, the bone, the flesh just as easily.

When will love's last kiss come? When will lovers last embrace?

Death at dawn is not exactly expected.

Night is when death feasts. And night is mostly when Clyde keeps vigil. But dawn finds him lightly asleep next to his Bonnie.

Gunfire stays the dream Clyde has been having wherein he is in leg irons shuffling down prison corridors with hands reaching for him through steel bars, with crude cat-calls ringing in his ears. And he sees in that last startling moment, just as the window of the cabin shatters, the ravenous eyes of Chicago Willy.

Screams and curses.

It's the laws!

Not again!

Yes, yes.

The racket of gunfire is real, is surreal.

But this is where Clyde is his coolest.

Clyde gives orders.

Fires back.

The world of laws and outlaws clash and test one another's resolve.

Bonnie watches her Clyde in action as he bravely (or foolishly) withstands the storm of bullets, which this time is even worse than in Joplin.

Everyone suffers a little blood loss, Buck especially — two in the head.

"Everyone pull the trigger!" Clyde commands.

Then somehow, miraculously, they are all in the sedan together, rushing past the armored car with the deputy inside shot in both knees, cursing: "Goddamn, goddamn," and racing toward yet another pitiless horizon even as all the DeSoto's glass is shattered in a squalor of gunfire.

Oh, it's bad, that's for sure, Clyde observes when at last he finds a safe back road and stops. He and W.D. make crude beds of old clothes and newspapers there on the dry grass on which they lay poor Buck and poor Bonnie, who is barely bleeding but with her leg still healing and afire.

Buck is a different story, dazed and dying. Blanche all weepy, calling him Daddy. Saying, "Please don't die on me, Daddy. Please don't die."

"This is bad," Clyde says to no one in particular.

There is a little meandering stream to their left — a cornfield with green stalks taller than a man to their right. It is a bucolic little field in which these birds have landed. Pretty and peaceful, which is something they all could stand a little of.

And all that day they nurse one another like a small ragged army of soldiers, bloody wounds and dazed thoughts.

And in the night crickets chirp with relentless rhythm and something moves through the corn causing its dry leaves to crackle. Coon maybe. The sky is flung with stars over the cold exhausted little encampment.

"What will we do, honey?" Bonnie asks.

But Clyde has no answer for her this time.

"Buck . . ." she starts to whisper.

"I know," Clyde says.

"Poor Blanche."

"Poor everyone."

The air becomes as cool as a basement and they huddle together, coats for blankets. Buck talks haphazardly of mysterious events in his delirium, while Blanche continues to call him Daddy.

W.D. shivers alone, but not just from the night air.

It is worse than he could have ever

imagined, this life of crime. The cops keep getting closer. The bullets keep getting closer. His very life feels like it is attached to a short string. Jesus, he's bleeding from three places already. It hurts. The cool air makes it hurt worse. His bones feel like they're trying to shake free of him, run away and leave the rest of him behind. His tooth hurts. Goddamn, of all the problems he's got, his fucking tooth hurts.

Daylight finds them still weary. Clyde places Bonnie in the DeSoto, tells the others he is going to scout the area for escape routes. All are too weary and wounded to care.

"It feels bad, honey," Bonnie says as Clyde drives slowly over the rough terrain.

"It will get better."

"I can't believe they came and shot us up again."

"What'd you expect?"

Clyde looks for routes of escape.

Eventually, shadows encroach as the sun falls once more into the creek. Unbeknownst to the little troupe are armed men creeping about — men accustomed to shooting squirrels, hare, a raiding fox now and then, but never another human being.

"Easy now," whispers the law. "Go easy, we don't want to give away our position."

Jug-eared farmers listen well.

"We going to do our civic duty is all I can say," one old man with a loose wattle of skin tells a reporter. "Gone help the law put an end to the Barrow Gang."

"I understand there are women with them. You up to shooting a woman if you have to?" the reporter asks.

"I reckon if it comes to it."

The reporter asks the farmer his name, as he is writing his deadline inside his head already: *The camp of the evildoers was surrounded by a hundred well-armed men of local flavor . . .*

"It don't never mind what my name is," the farmer says.

All are well prepared to shoot to kill. When posed with the question as to whether or not he could shoot the notorious Bonnie Parker if given the opportunity, a posse member was quoted as saying yes.

Everyone settles down to wait for the next day to break.

It is one long night. The rabbits don't know they are all but trapped.

Clyde presses himself against Bonnie. The warmth and the rhythm of her breathing are a comfort to him.

She is breathing a prayer:

Lord, don't let them kill Clyde and me . . .

183

17

Slaves to Love

Journal entry: *Oh, the next morning's gunplay was terrible. Men in coveralls shot into us. They showed no mercy whatsoever. They did their best to pick us off, and mostly they did. Buck was shot again and W.D. became lost in the fracas. Clyde and me escaped through the creek bed and into the cornfield, though not unscathed . . .*

"Run for your life," Clyde seethes.

Her shoes ruined already, Bonnie runs barefoot through the corn holding on to Clyde's belt, her dress torn, muddy.

Lucky for us, we came across the farmhouse when we did . . .

Making no bones about it, Clyde holds the unsuspecting farmer and his wife at bay saying, "Give me the keys to your automobile and this can all go easy."

It was as though we planned it, but we didn't. I know Clyde felt bad for leaving Buck behind. But nothing could be done and tears will have to wait to flow. We drove all day and night like mad. Bonnie Parker.

"We got two of the birds," one of the posse states with a mixture of pride and disappointment — "but we didn't get them all."

The last words Buck Barrow hears are: "Please don't die, Daddy . . ."

News comes over the radio: "Buck Barrow, brother of the now infamous Clyde Barrow of Bonnie and Clyde notoriety, is dead of wounds suffered in a gun battle with law enforcement officers . . ." and so on and so forth.

Clyde cusses the government bastards who did this.

"I promised Mother I'd always take care of him and if anything ever happened, I'd bring him home . . ." Clyde's words sound so fatal. Bonnie quotes him in her journal along with descriptions of their narrow escape.

There is a photograph in the *Dallas Morning News* of Blanche being held by deputies. In it, she is wearing riding britches — jodhpurs — struggling to get free, to get to her dying "Daddy." She looks like a debutante who has lost her horse, her stallion, her steed.

Clyde imagines Buck's struggle for every

breath, shot through and through as he was — nearly dead already when they shot him again — those government bastards.

Well, he'll write some names on his own bullets and see that they get sent to the right parties.

This season is changing. Rain washes away everything but memory, it seems. Listen to the way the rain runs down the walls. See the way the wind has begun to strip the trees bare. Feel the fallow breath of coming winter. Oh, but the seasons of both land and soul are becoming shorter and shorter.

Ted Hinton has a heart full of mixed feelings when he does read of the latest escape of Bonnie and Clyde; the two seem struck from metal no fire can melt, seem struck into a coin no lawman can pocket.

Perhaps it is why God created him, put him on this earth in this time and in this place — to bring about an end to the tragic lovers' endless good fortune. What an odd sense it gives him to think he could be the instrument of Bonnie Parker's death. He is not an especially religious man, but the comparison between himself and Judas is not so difficult to conjure. Well, wasn't that fellow preordained to bring down the *One whom he loved?* The way Ted sees it, he has no more choice in the matter than old Judas did.

He envisions the final scene played out wherein he plants a farewell kiss on the young beauty's dying lips — a kiss full of betrayal and desire. And in her last bit of *raison d'être* she will understand and forgive him his transgression.

But still, it seems a harsh and heavy role God should place on him when it could just as easily have been ordained that he and Bonnie Parker became more than mere friends — more than a waitress serving a postman pie and coffee five days a week. He sits slightly stunned at such thoughts.

"Well," Bob says, reading the same newspaper article, seeing the same distraught Blanche fighting to get to her dying husband (who in the photograph cannot even be seen for the number of posse members surrounding his supine and stricken body), "they shot the wrong Barrow, it seems to me. But a Barrow is a Barrow, and there is one less of them now."

"They seem to have uncommon luck for slipping the trap, sir," Ted says.

"Maybe so, but luck is as faithless as a streetwalker, son. Trust me. Their luck won't last that much longer."

Ted hefts the weight of a handful of unspent bullets, each the size of a pinkie finger.

Not much more than this is the weight of life itself.

A Dr Pepper bottle with a note inside is hastily flung from a speeding Ford. It lands with a thud on the dead grass lawn of the peaceful Barrows — a signal that Bonnie and Clyde are back in Dallas and ready for a family meeting.

The note says simply: *They are cooking red beans tonight at the usual place.*

Preparations are made. Food is packed into a basket along with hot chocolate — Clyde's favorite.

Emma Parker is notified by phone.

They are cooking red beans tonight at the usual place.

Oh, Lord, she can't wait to see her baby again and puts on a new dress she was planning to wear to church come Sunday.

For all know now of the fatal fight and how the odds have come to shift in favor of the law and how precious and few family reunions might become in such uncertain times.

It is a somber occasion what with Buck's

demise and Blanche's incarceration.

"She won't sing," says the elder Barrow, Henry. "She's a good woman."

"It'd be hard for her to sing since we never made any plans for her to tell the laws where we'd go next," Clyde agrees. "It's best nobody knows what my next move is."

"And how are you doing, honey?" Mama Emma asks her darling daughter whose eyes do look weary and full of the road.

"I'm okay," Bonnie says with a squeeze. "Me and Clyde are doing okay, Mama."

Down the lane the two of them walk for a little privacy.

"I wish you'd give yourself up, Bonnie."

"They'd put us in the electric chair."

"They wouldn't a girl like you. Just tell them you were forced, is all. They'd believe you."

"It wouldn't be right to betray Clyde like that."

"To hell with Clyde Barrow," Mama Emma seethes. "It's you I'm worried about. I can't stand by and see them kill you . . ."

"It's too late for any of that anyway. The die's been cast, Mama."

"No it isn't, honey. No it isn't."

★ ★ ★

They bid good-bye long after evening shadows have crept long over the land. Mama Emma drinks herself to sleep in the empty little house. Her night is long and fraught with worry and she misses church the next morning asleep in her new dress.

"It looks so pretty on you, Mama," Bonnie did comment when she saw it.

And as the morning unwinds and re-winds, the radio there in the kitchen is full of Jimmy Rogers and Billy Sunday preaching up a storm, his shrill voice giving plenty of notice to sinners about the *End Days,* about justice riding a white horse and swinging a sword — about lakes of fire!

"Oh, be quiet you son of a bitch!" she cries, then feels herself empty inside as her hand fumbles for the bottle.

Sun peeks through lead-colored clouds and sparkles in puddles turning them into mirrors in old cotton fields.

"I bet if you listened hard enough you could still hear the old slaves singing," Bonnie says somewhere between Dallas and Granbury.

"Old slaves, new slaves, we're all the same," remarks Clyde.

190

"Not you and me, honey. We're free, white, and twenty-one," Bonnie says, laughing. It is her child's quality to laugh in the face of anything Clyde so adores. Good old Bonnie who doesn't know the price of blood.

"We sure ain't free," Clyde mutters around his cigarette, for poverty has always been his master and his people's master.

"Where we headed, honey?"

"I wish I knew."

They stop and rob a Sinclair station and Clyde makes the clerk put a new battery in the Ford before cutting the telephone cord to the wall phone.

"Man, I wish you hadn't gone and done that," the clerk says when Clyde cuts the cord. "Mr. Rollins will come back and make me pay for all this stole stuff and that cord too."

Clyde hands the clerk a five-dollar bill, says, "Then you best not be here when he gets back."

The man looks pop-eyed.

"Go on, take it."

"Naw, I couldn't. It's Mr. Rollins's money."

"No, it's my money. It used to be his, now it's mine. That's the way things work."

The clerk shakes his head.

"I still got to live 'round here. You best go on before Mr. Rollins shows back up."

"You know who we are?" Clyde says.

The clerk nods.

"Yes sir, I believe I do."

"Then you make sure and tell Mr. Rollins who it was robbed you. Tell him Clyde Barrow says he best be careful about blaming the wrong people."

Later Bonnie asks, "Why do you think that Negro man wouldn't take the money, Clyde?"

"Because he's still a slave in his mind."

They order hamburgers and beer at a roadhouse south of Granbury, sleep that night in a motor court in a room that is musty with the dampness of Texas winter settling in. Even the sheets feel damp they are so cold.

Bonnie feels lonely. Bonnie feels in need of some attention. But when she reaches to touch Clyde, he seems to shrink.

"I'm beat, ain't you?" he says.

The hour is seven o'clock, the sky already dark.

"I guess, a little," she says.

He can hear the disappointment in her voice. He always knows exactly what she's feeling by the tone of her voice — it grows small, childish when she's disappointed.

"Aw, don't be that way, okay?"

"I feel like a slave," she says. "A slave to love and to you and to the whole world. I feel like that Negro at the filling station."

"You don't know anything about it."

Clyde puts forth his best effort and later they lie in the clammy room entangled in the clammy sheets, Bonnie's craving unfulfilled.

"It's just that I'm beat," Clyde says again.

"I know you are, honey. You've been driving like crazy. Everything's so crazy what's happened to us lately."

"The road," he says. "Being on the run all the time. It takes it out of you after a while."

"I know it."

"If we could just hit a place with enough money to get us on down to Mexico — down where it's warm and sunny all the time . . ."

The flame of the match that Clyde strikes off the headboard to light their cigarettes dances in their wet eyes.

"It might not be heaven," Bonnie says as Clyde snaps out the match, "but I'd rather be here with you than anyplace I know of."

"Me too," he says.

Clyde dreams of a big score.

Bonnie writes a new poem in her head: "Slaves to Love."

18

Love's Blue

Ted Hinton reads reports of robberies and other crimes committed all over Texas. In the reports are nearly always the same two names: Bonnie and Clyde.

"How can they be everywhere at once?"

Bob Alcorn says, "It's the in thing, didn't you know, to get robbed by Bonnie and Clyde. I'm surprised the victims aren't asking to have their pictures taken with them even as they're getting guns stuck in their kissers."

In a moment of clarity, call it an epiphany if you will, Ted Hinton's heart has turned cold. He has gone from longing and desire for the little vixen, to steely resolve to bring to a close this chapter — the final chapter of her sweet little life. Clyde has turned her feral. He's ruined her. It is a bittersweet conclusion that harkens Ted to load his guns. If she were my dog turned rabid, I'd shoot her. I've no choice. The sooner I accept that, the better everyone will be.

"I aim to put a stop to them," he tells Bob Alcorn.

Bob thumbs back his cattleman's hat.

"Hell, son, we get the chance, we'll knock 'em over like ducks at a shooting gallery."

Ted hears the rifle's crack, the metallic ping as the bullet glances off the little steel ducks that go 'round and 'round.

"Their game has become a sideshow," Ted says.

"A very dangerous sideshow," Bob adds. "And so far us police have looked like a bunch of rubes."

And later while walking the streets alone, Ted remembers this woman whose husband is a traveling salesman — a woman he used to deliver the mail to. She would sometimes invite him in for a cup of coffee. Her name is Agnes and she isn't very pretty and a bit overweight. And in those moments of miscellaneous conversation over Agnes's somewhat weak coffee, Ted felt her loneliness but steered clear of any entanglements for many reasons. But now that he has resolved to become a different man, Ted finds himself there on the sidewalk before Agnes's house.

The driveway is empty. Agnes spoke often of the long drives Mr. Maxwell would have to make just to sell his product — ball bearings. Why, all the way to St. Louis and Oklahoma City, gone for days at a time.

A single light shines there in the living room where, after several minutes, Ted sees Agnes's silhouette pass back and forth. There are three children, but at this hour surely they would be asleep in their beds. The dormer windows are dark.

What a fool I am, Ted thinks even as he climbs the stoop and gently knocks on the door with no ready story of why he is here at this late hour.

But when the door opens, Agnes simply looks at him for a moment before stepping aside to allow him entrance and leads him to a back room where there is a small cot and a single chair. It seems an odd but convenient sanctuary to retreat to from the empty world.

"Should I turn on the light or leave it off?" Agnes asks, the light from the hallway falling partway into the room.

"Off," he says.

Then without further conversation they proceed to undress.

Afterward Ted is tempted to ask her if

she's done this sort of thing before, and if so, how often, but realizes it is none of his business. There is never any talk of a repeat performance. He is sure that Agnes is a simple sort of girl who takes life as it is presented to her. With a passionless kiss on her warm cheek, they part wordlessly, and Ted once more enters the womb of night understanding for the first time how simple life can become.

"The water in the Gulf of Mexico is as blue as the sky," Bonnie says. "And you don't even have to know how to swim — all that salt in the water makes it easy for you to float."

"You saying nobody's ever drowned in the Gulf of Mexico?"

She is uncertain.

"Because if anybody's ever drowned in it, then you'd need to know how to swim — all that salt water wouldn't do you no good."

This conversation takes place over liverwurst sandwiches with sliced onions and mayonnaise washed down with Schlitz beer. There on the coffee table next to the sandwiches and beer are plans to break Ray Hamilton out of Huntsville Prison, the Eastham section.

"I don't see why we can't just go to the Gulf and find us a nice little cottage to stay in," Bonnie says. "Spend the winter and lay low."

"Look, I know you don't like Ray very much," Clyde says. "But he's a good crook and I could stand working with a good crook again. No more kids for me, no sir."

"Why risk getting ourselves killed over the guy?"

"Because no matter what we do, we risk getting killed. You got a thing or two to learn about loyalty, Bonnie."

She is wounded by such comments. Nobody has been more loyal than she.

"My love does not hesitate," she says, making her voice sharp as a knife's edge.

"What's that supposed to mean? I don't know when you say stuff like that what it is supposed to mean?"

"You can be awfully damn stupid-headed!"

He looks up from the plans he's preparing to rescue Ray Hamilton — crude drawings of roads and buildings with times and dates written down on pieces of lined notebook paper. A Chesterfield smolders in a clay ashtray. The plan according to Ray, who has pretty much worked it out, isn't that complicated. But Clyde obsesses, wanting to make sure the risks are minimized.

"Now I know what *that* means," he says, rising aggressively from the overstuffed chair.

"Go on. You want to take a swing at me — go on!"

Cat-quick he is across the room and has her by the wrists, his face a flourish of anger.

"I wonder sometimes why the hell I ever brought you along!"

"Yeah, I wonder that too — you never even fuck me anymore."

He slaps her hard and she tumbles back onto the sofa she'd been sitting on reading detective magazines. Her mouth turns two shades of red: one from her lipstick, the other from the blood of a split lip.

She seems mesmerized by the sight of her own blood there on the fingertips she uses to swab her mouth.

Clyde shakes like a man with palsy.

"Oh, Christ, honey!" he says. "I didn't mean to . . ."

She knows his potential for sudden violence. But this is the first time he's turned on her.

It is neither the sting of his blow, nor fear of him, however, that causes her to burst into tears. It is a deeper, more frightening feeling that overcomes her.

Clyde tries to console her.

She insists on him taking her home to her mother.

He insists that she stay with him.

"It's no good anymore," she sobs.

"Yes it is. It's no good for me if you leave me."

He begs, he cajoles, he makes every conceivable argument to retain her. Running through her mind are a thousand reasons to want to leave.

"I'd just as soon the laws shoot me as to be without you," he pleads.

She is regrettably lonely for her previous life, the one she thinks of as *BC* — Before Clyde.

"I wanted to make something of myself," she sobs. "I wanted to be somebody. I didn't want to have to hurt anyone."

He pulls his hair, crumples beside her, fallen to his knees like a novitiate seeking acceptance into a world not of his own making. He wants so much to be in that world Bonnie is always dreaming about — that bright world where everyone is always happy, where poems are composed, songs sung, and neon glows all through the night so that it is never dark or lonely.

"Don't leave me, baby. Don't leave me," he begs and begs.

Until he feels the dainty hand upon his head . . .

Until he looks up into her luminous forgiving eyes . . .

Until the pouting swollen mouth offers him a Madonna's smile . . .

"I said a hateful thing to you, honey. I didn't mean it."

"It don't matter, baby. It don't matter as long as you don't leave me."

"I won't leave you, Clyde. I could never leave you."

It is a lot easier than they thought to break Ray Hamilton out of Eastham.

"Texas cops are a lot better at catching a fellow than keeping him," Ray says breathlessly once he is riding down those harsh back roads again with Bonnie and Clyde. Joining the little troupe as well, a fellow escapee, Henry Methvin, a man Bonnie judges to be only slightly less attractive than a swamp toad.

Ray talks incessantly about how good his plan was to break them out of the prison.

"Pretty slick, eh? Waiting till me and Henry here got sent out on a timber-cutting party."

"Yeah, yeah," Clyde agrees, already half sorry he is rejoined with the mouthy Ray who seems to be a bigger braggart than before.

And what's with the other guy, Henry? Ray hadn't said anything about bringing along another guy. And this Henry is quiet and doesn't say anything, just stares out the window.

"Head toward Wichita Falls," Ray says, once Clyde has steered them past all the possible roadblocks taking a dozen Texas back roads.

"What's in Wichita Falls?" Clyde says.

"I got to see somebody there."

"We're not on some picnic, Ray."

"This is somebody important, I assure you."

The somebody proves to be a woman named Mary, the wife of one of Ray's former partners who is serving fifty years in jail. "Fifty years is a very long time to wait for love," Ray says, laughing. The next anyone knows, Mary is tossing her suitcase in the trunk of the car.

"Jesus Christ, you guys got more guns in here than an army," Mary says.

It is enough to set everyone on edge, this Mary's mouth that is almost as big as Ray's.

Then getting into the car, Mary reaches her hand over the front seat and says to Bonnie, "Glad to meet cha." And, "It's nice to know I'm not the only dame alone

202

with these three mugs." Laughs in a loud way. Bonnie rolls her eyes at Clyde.

That night at a motor court, in the confines of their small room, Bonnie says as Clyde undresses, "Ours is a life of repetition. It feels like we've done this a thousand times before."

"It won't be this way forever."

"What makes you think not? I mean what do you see happening here, Clyde, that hasn't happened a million times already? Jesus, honey, I'd like to get off this Ferris wheel."

"We'll go to Fort Worth tomorrow and buy some new clothes. How'd you like that?"

"I don't like Ray and I don't like Mary. That Henry guy doesn't say boo. I don't like him either. Buying a couple of new dresses isn't going to change anything in my book."

Bonnie sits on the edge of the bed in just her slip and hose.

Clyde places a hand on her back, rubs her neck a little.

"It's going to be okay. We'll hit some good places, make us some money, then split for Mexico, like you wanted. We'll go wade in the goddamn Gulf . . ." He tries to make light of things. "But I ain't going in over my head . . ."

"Promise me," Bonnie says.

"Sure, honey. Let's just try getting along with everyone till then, okay? Let's keep a stiff upper lip. Ain't you the one always looking at the bright side of things?"

"She snorts when she laughs," Bonnie says. "You hear her? It's irritating as hell."

If Clyde didn't know different, he'd think Bonnie was a little jealous of Mary who really isn't all that hard on the eyes.

"It doesn't bother me as much as you," Clyde says, shaking a cigarette loose from his pack. "I just wish that Henry would say something once in a while."

Clyde turns out the overhead light. Lies down on the bed. He shows little interest in her. Bonnie figures he probably is beat from the long hours of driving, that he's got a lot on his mind now that he has a new gang together. She thinks back on that afternoon with her and Ray. She hopes Ray doesn't start shooting his mouth off about it. Ray spent all afternoon there in the backseat with Mary bragging about all the jobs he pulled, what a smart guy he is. Mary all the time kissing his face and neck, cuddling and cooing. Ray likes to put the horns to Clyde, telling him they ought to start pulling some real jobs, no more gas stations or grocery stores. For whatever reason, Clyde lets Ray get away with it. At least for now.

"I love you," she says.

"I love you too," he says.

She waits there in the dark, hears the burn of his cigarette.

Farther out, they can hear the road traffic, less now that night has fallen. Occasionally headlights sweep the walls as an automobile pulls into the motor court. Clyde doesn't say anything, but she knows he's alert, listening, prepared to leap from the bed guns in hand.

That thing she said to him the other day in anger, she wonders if he's thinking about that as he keeps vigil for the law. If he had said it to her instead, she'd be thinking about it all the time. It would hurt like hell.

She reaches out and touches him, feels him stiffen, the knot of muscle there along his forearm thick as the body of a snake ready to strike.

"It's okay," she whispers.

The muscle relaxes.

"I'm bushed," he says, then stubs out his cigarette and rolls over on his side, his back to her. "We got a full day ahead of us tomorrow, better get some sleep."

But she cannot sleep so easily. Instead

she imagines how warm the water in the Gulf of Mexico is as it swirls up around her legs, slithers past her hips, touches her breasts.

There is something aimless and dreamy about it.

A caressing sea of blue water that washes away her blue mood.

19

Bridging Love's Troubled Waters

The Wabash River don't look anything like the Red, does it?"

Clyde throws out the question to no one in particular as he drives across the iron bridge into Terre Haute, its gray stone buildings rising from the far bank, lifting out of a fog that will soon give way to an early spring sun.

Henry Methvin is dozing in the backseat, his face pressed to the window, his hat tipped crookedly over one eye. Ray and Mary are up to their usual high jinks — giggling like a couple of high school kids. Grabbing each other under a blanket. Drinking homemade hooch. Clyde glances in the rearview mirror at Ray. *Gangster my ass*, he thinks.

They find a hotel, a kidney red brick building six stories tall in the heart of downtown. Take the elevator up to the fifth floor, a bellboy carrying their suitcases —

one of which contains guns.

"This is nice," Bonnie says once implanted into her and Clyde's room. Clyde is already looking out the window. The bellboy stands there. Bonnie takes a quarter out of her purse and gives it to the kid. He looks at it, turns, and walks out without saying so much as a "thank you."

Clyde puts things in order — slides the suitcase with the guns under his side of the bed where he can reach it easy if he needs to. Bonnie looks out the window, tests the bedsprings by bouncing on the side of the bed before looking in the bathroom.

"Pretty swell," she says.

"Beats the backseat of a car, huh?"

"Sure does, or half those other joints we stayed in, like that place with the cement teepees, remember?"

"We never stayed in that place."

She thought they had.

"Thing is," Clyde says, "the laws catch us way up here, we got no escape route." Says this looking out the window again, at how high up they are. Nobody would survive a jump this high up.

Bonnie is eager to test the bed for real.

"You want to?" she says, sliding on top of the covers.

Clyde lights a cigarette, removes his

jacket, drapes it over the back of a chair. There is a radiator painted white just below the window.

"I thought maybe you and Mary'd want to go shopping or something," Clyde says.

"We can do that whenever. Come on, honey."

Well, what the hell, it's still early and there doesn't look like there is a lot to do in the sleepy-looking town. Terre Haute looks pretty tame, like a place you'd grow old in.

"Sure, okay," he says and comes over and stands at the side of the bed.

Bonnie slides closer to him, her dress riding up past her knees.

"Kiss me," she says. "I want to be real romantic, this is such a swell place . . ."

He kisses her. Her tongue is small and warm and darts inside his mouth. He wishes it would turn him on more, this stuff.

She runs her hands over the front of him.

"That's it," he says, hoping.

"Like this?" she says.

"Yeah, just like that."

She undoes his belt. He closes his eyes, leans back, lets her do what she's doing, and tries not to think of being back in

Eastham that time before he cut his toes off.

Later she says, "Now my turn, honey."

He doesn't mind so much. What the hell, what else you going to do in a place like Terre Haute before lunch?

Mary tries to plant the bug in Bonnie's ear while they're shopping for dresses in a department store. Bonnie is trying on a red jersey dress, white buttons down the front, tan trim.

"I notice you and Clyde don't seem to get along too well lately," Mary says, one foot on a chair while she straightens the seam of her nylons.

"It's just lately," Bonnie says, watching herself in the mirror, the way the dress clings to her slender body, Mary over her shoulder not ashamed at all to be strutting her stuff right there in the same dressing room.

"Yeah, well, if I were you, I'd dump the grump. Life's too short not to have a lot of laughs. That's what I like about Ray, he's always up for a good laugh."

"Clyde's the more serious type. He always has been."

"Listen, kiddo, it ain't none of my business, really. But you know, you always got choices you can make. You don't have to stay with the guy."

"What's that supposed to mean?"

Mary finishes her adjustment but doesn't change position except to turn her face enough so she can look at Bonnie looking at her there in the mirror.

"Ray's a real fun guy," Mary says. "He's enough guy for two women if you catch my drift."

It takes a moment to sink in.

"You wouldn't mind sharing him with another woman?"

"Nah. I ain't the jealous type. Life's just a bowl of cherries."

Then finally standing up, Mary moves a little closer to Bonnie, maybe a little too close, says, "In fact, I'm just the opposite of the jealous type."

Then adds: "Say, that dress looks real nice on you, kid. Goes good with your figure."

It is not until Ray starts making passes at her too that Bonnie begins to think: *Conspiracy.*

Life flows as lazy as the Wabash for the next couple of weeks.

Bonnie tries to ignore Ray and Mary, tries to play coy, tries to play dumb when

Ray makes offhanded comments about how she should think maybe of "bumping off old Clyde" and running away with him and Mary.

"You could slip something in his food," Ray says with a laugh one time when Bonnie got into it with Clyde over something she can't even remember. Angry, Clyde goes out for a drive alone — his solace is only found behind the steering wheel of a Ford V-8 it seems.

"Who would know if you were to slip a little rat poison in his food?" Ray says.

"I'd know," Bonnie says. "And I'd like it if you and Mary would leave off me, okay!"

Ray looks at her with that look that says, *Remember that time you and me . . .* But Bonnie shoots him a look that says, *Remember what I said, how I'd figure out a way to kill you, or get Clyde to kill you?*

And after that it is finished between them, all this crazy talk, the flirting around.

After that Ray and Mary act real snotty to her. And Ray is always harping on Clyde about what a small thinker he is for always wanting to stick up filling stations and grocery stores instead of banks.

Oddly enough Clyde doesn't even act mad when Ray says these things to him.

Then one time Ray is drunk, Mary is too. It's the middle of the day and they've just finished having lunch at this nice little Italian restaurant and Ray calls Clyde a punk. But Clyde acts as though he doesn't even hear what Ray says. Instead he gets up and goes to pay the tab for all their meals and they walk outside together. And just when they're getting into the car Clyde hits him, the roll of quarters Clyde bought from the hostess balled up in his fist.

It sounds like hardly nothing at all, just a smack, but Bonnie sees the way Ray's cheekbone looks caved in when he pulls himself up to his knees using the door handle of the sedan for leverage.

Clyde hits him again, same spot, quick and hard, and Ray goes down again, this time leaking blood from his mouth, maybe his nose too, the blood dripping on the curb.

This time Ray only raises his head, looks up at them. Mary starts to reach down to help him but Clyde pushes her aside, says to her, "Get in the car, don't try and help him."

Ray's mouth is moving as though he is testing to see if his jaw is broken. Clyde opens the back door of the sedan, says, "Get in the car."

Once they are all in the car, Clyde looks in the rearview mirror, sees Ray is holding a hankie Mary gave him to his face, the hankie soaking up blood till it drips down over his fingers.

"Don't ever call me a punk again," Clyde says, starting the engine. "Fact, don't ever call me anything again."

Ray just looks at him, the handkerchief a bloody rag.

"And don't ever make a play for my girl again, either of you." Shifting the gear lever smoothly into first.

Ray and Mary leave sometime in the middle of the night. Bonnie hears a door across the hall slam, goes to the window and looks down until she sees the two of them exiting the hotel's front door, a yellow cab there at the curb waiting for them.

She is glad they are gone. She hopes Ray gets picked up again by the law and put away for good. She hopes Clyde has learned his lesson about Ray Hamilton. She sure has.

The next morning, Clyde cools his knuckles in a bowl of ice cubes he has the bellman bring up. Henry Methvin is sitting in an armchair across from him and Bonnie, silent as a sphinx.

"Your partner flew the coop last night," Clyde says. "You want to join him, now's the time."

Henry has the eyes of a man not fully awake.

"Me and him were never that close," he says.

"How would you feel about being part of the Barrow Gang?"

Henry looks at Clyde, then at Bonnie.

"I guess," he says.

"Better than sitting in stir, right?"

"Right."

"You okay with this?" Clyde asks Bonnie.

"Why ask me?" she says.

Clyde looks at Henry.

"Me and her, we're equal partners. You understand?"

"Sure," Henry says. "What's not to understand."

Clyde and Bonnie decide it is not such a good thing to stay around Terre Haute.

"Ray's mad enough and rotten enough to call the cops on us," Clyde says.

Bonnie knows that Clyde beating Ray up isn't the only reason Ray would have for getting even with Clyde. There are other reasons too. Reasons from before.

Passion turns to hatred sometimes, maybe

more often than any of us would like to think, she muses, thinking about a poem she wants to write as she and Clyde and Henry Methvin head west again. The muddy waters of the Wabash River can be seen through the iron grating of the bridge they cross — a river and a bridge that lead both ways, like the heart sometimes does.

Go on, river, just like me and Clyde will keep doing. We'll just go on until we can't anymore. Isn't that what Clyde always says.

20

A White Rabbit to Show My Love

They're cooking red beans tonight at the bone yard.

"It's so nice and peaceful here," Bonnie says as they wait for their families to arrive.

Henry Methvin is walking among the headstones, reading the names and dates of when people were born and when they died. He calculates in his head how old they were. He wonders if the diggers measure exactly how far down six feet is, or do they just guess.

The weathered oaks are not leafed out yet. Spring is slow this year. The sky is smudged, unhappy, silent.

Several of the headstones are of polished granite, pink and smooth as glass. But most are simple, rough slabs the long seasons have stained to the point it seems they've wept black tears. A steady wind blows down from the north, cold, like it is coming straight out of the Texas Panhandle. Clyde sniffs the air thinking he'll even catch a whiff of cow shit. He doesn't.

Pretty soon a pair of automobiles appear on the road leading to the wrought-iron archway, then slowly pass through and drive up to where the trio has parked. Clyde has left the motor of his V-8 running just in case it isn't family coming to visit.

Kin pile out of the two automobiles, almost cautiously they approach one another, then hug and say their how-dos and slap each other on the back.

The home folks hate to see their infamous kin like this, always in some out of the way place, always under the air of secrecy. Henry Methvin stays off by himself, not wanting to meet anyone new. Clyde explains about the guy walking around looking at the gravestones.

"Maybe he'd like some fried chicken," Cummie Barrow, Clyde's mother, says.

Clyde notices how worn her face has become, remembers how pretty and dark-haired she used to be. She is just skin and bones now, old-looking. His old daddy has lost youth, too. They used to be a lively pair, going off to Saturday night dances together, coming in the house afterward, laughing. That was before times got bad, before they had to go live under the viaduct and that sort of life started turning them old fast.

"Henry's a bit standoffish," Clyde explains. "We'll make up a plate and give it to him later on."

Mother Emma hugs Bonnie, heart full of bad premonition she'll never see her daughter again after this day — certain that meeting here in a cemetery is symbolic of darker times ahead.

"Why'd you two choose this place for us to meet in?" she asks her pretty little daughter.

"Clyde thought the laws would never look for us in a graveyard, Mama."

"He's right. Only the devil would look for you here. It gives me the heebie jeebies."

The women soon make a spread there on the hoods of the cars: fried chicken, biscuits, potato salad, jars of sweet tea. Everyone eats standing up, gathered around the automobiles, the wind riffling through their hair, lifting the skirts of the women who brush them down again, the men in hats and shirtsleeves.

Henry gazes down at a headstone with three names on it. Two of the names have no date; they just say *Infant*. Henry wonders if they knew they died, or was it just like they never knew anything.

After their meal, the men smoke cigarettes and ask Clyde what his plans are as Bonnie and her mother take a walk together in the opposite direction of where Henry is looking at markers.

"Where you heading this time, old son?" Clyde's daddy asks, squinting through a cloudy mask of cigarette smoke.

"Don't know. Me and Bonnie just keep on going, that's all," Clyde says with a lopsided smile.

Somehow it doesn't equate with the old man who never could understand the need in his boys to go wrong. One already lost to gunplay, and Clyde most likely too, soon enough. He cuts his gaze toward Bonnie walking with her mama, feeling just as sad for her because he's come to love her like true kin.

"You know they'd probably stop looking for you two if you was to go down to Mexico, or even up to Canada," his daddy says.

"I don't think they'll ever let us rest until they kill us, Daddy. They put too many charges against us."

Cummie wraps her arms around Clyde's neck, her tears dropping cold on his cheek.

"I wish . . . I wish . . ." she says before she is overcome and her husband puts a bony arm around her shoulders and leads her off.

Clyde stuffs his hands down inside his pockets, feels loose change — some standing buffalo nickels and Indian head pennies. Henry Methvin chooses this time to look at the bunch of them gathered around the automobiles. His and Clyde's eyes meet across the expanse of the dead. Then Henry looks back down at the head-stone near his feet.

Hell of a thing, he thinks, looking at those names again, *not even to get a chance to drive a car or date a girl or nothing.*

Mama Emma says, "Get in the car with me when we go back. Drive off with me and let Clyde go, honey. I mean it . . ."

"I can't."

"Why can't you? Tell me one damn reason why you can't."

"Haven't we gone through this about a million times, Mama?"

"We'll go through it a million more if that's what it takes to talk some sense into your head."

"Don't. Let's not ruin our little bit of time together by arguing . . ."

Oh, it is like the weight of a gravestone upon Emma Parker, the grief that presses against her heart; that has been pressing there for months and months.

"Just answer me one thing, then. Where did I go wrong with you?"

"You didn't go wrong with me, Mama. Love is what went wrong with me."

Clyde reads the letter Ray Hamilton has written to the *Dallas Morning News* accusing him of murder and being a "Yellow Punk." Clyde reads the letter three more times. Lights a cigarette.

"I never set out in my life to kill anybody," he tells Henry Methvin who has been reading an article in *Master Detective*: Trapping the Murdering Monster of Fairmount Park.

Henry's turtle eyes blink.

"I read where you shot quite a few guys," Henry says. "You and Ray."

"I didn't shoot any guys just for the sake of shooting them. But I'm going to shoot that fucking Ray."

Henry doesn't know quite what to say.

"I'm going to kill him and you're going to help me."

And when Henry still doesn't say anything, Clyde asks, "You have a problem with that?"

"No, I don't have any problem with that. You want me to help you, then I'll help you. Me and him weren't ever that close."

"Good."

Clyde's good and mad.

He writes his own letter, shows it to Bonnie.

"There are some misspelled words in it, honey," she says.

"So what."

Clyde makes plans to assassinate Ray Hamilton.

"What if Mary O is with him when you catch up to him?" Bonnie asks. She hates Ray and she doesn't care much for Mary — but still, she doesn't want to see her dead or anything. She doesn't like the idea of Clyde shooting a woman.

Henry Methvin says, "You want, I'll take care of her," but doesn't say exactly what he means by this.

But everybody's problem is solved soon enough when they hear over the radio that very same week that Ray has been arrested just a little outside of Sherman. All that planning for nothing, Clyde thinks.

"You think he'll talk, try and cut a deal?" Henry says.

"Caged birds always sing," Clyde says.

Henry thinks Clyde is a pretty clever fellow to say such clever things.

The newspapers tell of Ray Hamilton's capture, of his betrayal by Mary O, who the police found living alone in Amarillo. Who the police say gave them information leading to the capture of her lover. Who is quoted as saying how she never did love the guy to begin with and so on and so forth . . .

Bonnie avidly reads of the newspaper account while Clyde and Henry clean guns, drink beer, eat sandwiches. She reads the account aloud at Clyde's request.

"Says here she told the police she was only along for the ride, that she only was with Ray for the high times . . . Says that when they picked up Ray, he was living like a hobo, riding freights. Says he told the police he was all out of bullets, whiskey, and women and that they might as well take him back to jail . . ."

"He's got a wise mouth," Clyde says, looking down the barrel of his pistol, happy they caught old Ray and happier still he was down and out when they caught him.

"He really say that about being out of whiskey and women?" Henry says, putting down a forty-five and picking up a bologna sandwich, the gun grease on his fingers soaking into the bread.

★ ★ ★

"Ted Hinton, like you to meet Frank Hamer and Manny Gault," Bob Alcorn says by way of introduction. Bob has gotten word from higher up they're sending down two ex Texas Rangers and full cooperation is needed and expected.

Frank stands tall in his high-heeled boots, Manny a head shorter.

Ted has been studying photographs of Bonnie and her Clyde: embraced, smoking cigars, pretending to be aiming guns at each other. Bonnie cute as a button acting like a real moll. Clyde's face captures shadows. Bonnie seems to attract all the light.

The one he likes best of her is the one she's wearing a beret. She looks pretty and tough, like an actress — or a singer maybe.

The two new men look down at the photographs. With fingertips they slide them across the table to each other.

"Just a couple of damn kids," Frank Hamer says, "is all it looks like to me."

"Kids that'll kill you in a heartbeat," Bob says. "Ask any of the poor bastards they've shot." The other new guy nods.

"They been like a pair of ghosts," Bob further decries. "Ghosts nobody can catch."

"Show me they can take a bullet through

their hearts and keep going and I'll agree with you," says Frank Hamer.

The former Rangers lay out their plans for setting a death trap, Frank Hamer doing most of the talking now, the butt of his gun peeking beneath his open jacket. Ted Hinton moves closer to the office window, stands so the sun can warm his face through the glass. Spring is about upon them all. Yesterday he saw crocuses trying to bloom in Mrs. Webster's yard. He's promised himself he wouldn't return, but had yet again. Only this time all they did was sit and talk over coffee and she told him she'd had a birthday the day before. He felt pretty bad about hearing it, how she'd spent the day alone.

"I've gotten used to it pretty much," she said, and he knew then he wouldn't ever go back to visit her again. Then when he left, he saw the pointed green tips of the crocuses poking through the still-damp earth there in her yard. He knew that in another few weeks they'd be in full bloom.

He is momentarily lost in the image of crocuses.

"What do you think, Ted?" Bob is asking him.

He doesn't even know what the question was.

★ ★ ★

Oh, the drive from Memphis to Dallas is a long one. Long and weary when you're on the dodge and sticking to the back roads and driving under moonlit nights. And so they do rest along the way, huddled in the backseat with coats for blankets and hats for pillows. Henry, the insomniac, stands guard, his turtle eyes never quite closing, never fully open.

He steps outside the car twice to relieve himself. Listens to the sound his piss makes falling like raindrops into the darkness of weeds. And next morning when the two policemen park their motorcycles there not distant from the somnolent warriors and start strolling in their curious fashion toward the black sedan, it is as much a surprise to Henry as anyone that he kills them both upon what he perceives as Clyde's command to "Let's take them."

It is only once Clyde's rage has subsided, when they are well away from that bloody scene, that Clyde himself does explain what he meant.

"Kidnap them, stupid!"

But Henry's nerves are worn thin and he only half listens.

"Damn it, honey," Bonnie says, petting the white rabbit she's bought her mother for Easter. She has named it "Hop."

Says Clyde, "It's just one more nail in our coffin."

Henry watches through the rear window scenery running in the opposite direction.

"You know I got some people in Louisiana," Henry says somewhat apologetically. "We could lay low there for a time if you want."

"What do you think?" Clyde asks Bonnie.

"The doors keep closing on us," she says. "Only we're the ones closing them, honey."

"I guess what's done is done."

"I guess maybe it is."

Clyde pets the rabbit in Bonnie's lap, its head bony and solid as a baseball beneath its white fur. Its pink startled eyes blinking.

21

Love's Divine Repast

I am a dark thread in Death's quilt.

No, that doesn't sound right.

Bonnie is trying to compose a poem in her head. She notices the spreading oaks with their Spanish moss standing watch, it seems.

"These are the bayous," Henry Methvin says from his perch in the backseat of the newly stolen tan Ford.

"It looks like the hair of dead belles hanging from their limbs," Bonnie says, speaking of the moss.

"There are lots of stories about this land," Henry concedes.

Clyde drives his usual fast style, a cigarette dangling from his lips. The place looks spooky to him, especially in the fading metal light. They stop once to stretch their legs and from deeper in the old trees comes a sound neither Bonnie nor Clyde have ever heard before.

"What's that?" Clyde says, reaching for the pistol in his belt.

Henry laughs, says it is the roar of a bull gator.

Clyde can see the thing in his mind — its jaws open, a mouthful of teeth. His feet feel itchy to get moving again.

"Fuck this," says he, getting back behind the wheel.

The sky over the swamps is the color of weathered tin. The trees turn into shadows as swamp swallows sun. The headlights of their car strike a crane standing in a water-filled ditch its feathers snow white. Its small eyes blink once as it lifts into flight.

On into the night they drive until they see a roadhouse not far down a macadam driveway, its parking lot full of automobiles and trucks. Music riffles through the stolid night air.

"We could stop and eat us a Po Boy," Henry says, remembering the taste from his boyhood.

"I hear they eat just about anything down in here," Clyde says, slowing the V-8, "including such things as opossums."

Henry laughs, says, "That's right, they do."

Bonnie makes a face.

Clyde pulls into the parking lot next to a

flivver with its rear bumper missing. He thinks this might be a good place to steal some license plates.

Folks are standing outside on the steps, smoking, talking, drinking out of Mason jars of illegal shine the local sheriff sells out of the trunk of his police car. For a man with many children, a wife, and a gal friend over in Arcadia needs to earn a little extra something above what the county pays.

Clyde looks 'round, but sees no current sign of the laws.

He hands Henry a few dollars, says, "Why don't you go get us some of those poor boys you're talking about."

"No, they're called Po Boys," Henry corrects, exiting the automobile.

Bonnie says, "It sounds like they're having quite a bit of fun inside."

Clyde tilts his head, listens through the open window. Bonnie likes the way he wears his hat at an angle, sometimes low over his eyes, like now.

"We could go in," she suggests.

"And do what?"

"Dance a little, maybe."

"You remember the last time we went dancing, what that ended up being?"

"Yes, honey, but what are the chances

the same thing will happen again?"

"Our luck is as poor as most these folks," Clyde says, nodding toward a gaggle of men standing near the front steps in their baggy, worn coveralls, their straw hats, smoking ready-mades and passing around a jar of the shine.

"Hell, I don't think we should risk being seen. They got rewards all over the place for us, Bonnie."

A few minutes later Henry walks up to the car and hands them the sandwiches through the window. The Po Boys are wrapped in wax paper. He hands them a couple of bottles of cold beer.

"Here you go," he says.

Bonnie and Clyde are famished.

"Say, these are pretty good," Clyde says after chewing on his and swallowing a mouthful.

"You can't beat Cajuns for their food," says Henry in a slightly exaggerated drawl.

The bread's been fried in grease.

Henry climbs into the backseat.

"How far to your daddy's?" Clyde says.

"Not that much farther, just outside Shreveport a little. Just keep on down this road a ways."

Bonnie is watching the men and women coming and going through the front door of the roadhouse. She sees how they hold on to each other, how sometimes they stop and kiss each other. She sees how happy and carefree they seem to be.

Wouldn't it be something if Clyde and me could just go out dancing on Saturday night, then go home to our bed, safe and sound, not having to worry about a thing. It is a thought that seems much more akin to a dream than to reality.

"What do you think of that sandwich, honey?" Clyde says.

"It's a little greasy."

"Hell, it's just about right, isn't it."

Clyde is feeling swell because they jumped the state line about half an hour ago. They're not wanted for any crimes in Louisiana, and even a Texas Ranger wouldn't cross a damn state line to catch somebody, no matter how bad he wanted to.

"They dancing inside, Henry?" Clyde asks.

"They sure are. Like a bunch of June bugs on a hot skillet."

"What sort of music is that?" Bonnie asks.

"Zydeco," says Henry.

"It makes you want to get up and shake something," Bonnie says playfully, poking Clyde in the ribs. He's got a dab of grease on his chin.

"Yeah," he says, teasing her like he sometimes does. "Shake what, pretty little mama?"

"This," she says, and wiggles her hips.

"That, huh?"

"Yeah, that and a whole lot more if a guy was to ask a girl the right way."

Clyde looks into the rearview mirror. Henry is back there with his hat notched back eating his poor boy sandwich. That's what it sounds like to Clyde — *Poor Boy*.

Clyde decides a little fun might be just the thing.

"Let's hit it," he says.

Bonnie squeals with glee, and all three pile out of the automobile and walk across the lot, the broken stones crunching under their shoes.

Inside, they shuffle over a sawdust floor to a band that plays guitars and fiddles and one guy brushing a washboard and another squeezing a concertina. The women are mostly dark-haired and dark-eyed and the men are too. They all shuffle 'round in a large wheel of humanity, the warm Louisiana night damp on their necks, damp on their cheeks. The music itself is rambunctious, untamed, wanton. The eyes of the dancers send silent messages to one another; messages of a need to forget hardships, messages of lust, and messages about the mysteries of the swamp and what they know about life here in the bayou.

A tall, skinny man sings in a lilting voice that sounds at times like a woman crying out in passion, sings in a bloody mix of French and English.

Clyde feels uneasy in this raw unbridled climate, but Bonnie is lost in the music and dances with her eyes closed, her body sweet and tender against him in a way that makes him want to forget where they are and who they are, and what lies ahead.

Clyde sees some of the men watching Bonnie with their dark eyes. Some of the women are watching, too. Bonnie, so fair-haired, is not one of them. Clyde could be. Henry most certainly is.

Before the night is over, Henry will show them how to eat crawdads, and Bonnie will be asked to dance by a stuttering man, and one of the fiddler's strings will break and he won't have another to replace it.

And sometime between that late hour and the first morning light, the swamp air will cool and the gator will hush its throaty roar, and a murky miasma will float over the stagnant waters appearing ahead of their headlights like skulking ghosts headed home from an evening of mischief.

All tired, they pull over to the side of the road and sleep.

Clyde awakes just as the policeman aims his gun at his face and pulls the trigger.

Only the crash is not of a policeman's revolver, but of a truck gone off the road and struck a tree.

He pulls himself free of Bonnie's slumbering body in time to see two black men climb out of the cab of the truck, one cursing the other, looking over the damage done. The truck is maybe ten yards farther up the road from where they are parked. Its radiator is hissing steam, its left front wheel collapsed.

There is a liquid red sun just above the hardwoods with enough heat to it to have burned off most of the night fog, but not all.

For whatever reason, Clyde feels sorry for the two hapless men. He walks over to where they are standing and scratching their heads assessing the damage done.

"You boys got a busted axle there."

The two men look at each other.

"Yes suh."

Suspicious of white strangers, especially ones in suit coats and wearing neckties and fedoras, they are pretty sure this fellow could possibly be some big city police from

Shreveport or maybe New Orleans. They ain't done nothing illegal, this much they know. But somehow this white fellow is making them feel as though they have.

Clyde straightens from looking down where the axle is busted.

That's when they see the pistol sticking down inside his belt — right then as he straightens up and his suit coat parts.

Clyde shakes his head.

"Looks like she's had it," says he.

"Yes suh."

Clyde looks up the road toward the direction the truck was headed before it hit the tree.

"Too bad we're not going your way or I'd give you boys a lift into town."

They reckon aloud that's all right. They can walk into town. They've done it before — lots of times.

"What are you hauling?" Clyde says, looking toward the back of the truck.

"Cantaloupes," says one.

"Cantaloupes. They any good this early?"

"They pretty good."

"How much would you charge me for one?"

"Twenty cents, you take your pick."

Bonnie, still rubbing sleep from her eyes,

watches from inside the automobile as Clyde buys a cantaloupe from the two black men and walks to the sedan carrying it in both hands.

"You ever see a cantaloupe this big?" he says proudly.

They eat it for breakfast.

Henry says, "Why didn't you just wait until those two niggers walked on down the road and then steal you one?"

"That's a good question," says Clyde. "I don't know."

Bonnie says, "Because Clyde and me know what it is to be poor, and it wouldn't be right to steal from somebody that's so damn poor is why he didn't."

"Oh," says Henry.

She's always sticking up for me, Clyde thinks proudly of his pretty Bonnie.

And later they turn on to a long dirt road Henry has directed them down at a juncture that seems more farmland than swamp and they drive along it for a few minutes before Henry instructs: "Here. Turn here."

There is a shed, its low roof sagged in the middle, and beyond it a small white house sitting up on blocks about as tall as a man's knee.

"This is where my daddy lives," Henry is pleased to inform.

Clyde likes the fact the house is situated out of sight from the main road. He sees no neighboring houses.

"This looks like a good place to lay low awhile, Henry."

Bonnie sees butterflies in a field of clover, says, "Oh, look."

Henry doesn't understand what the big deal is — he's seen plenty of butterflies.

Ted Hinton's eyes follow the path that Frank Hamer's forefinger makes across a map.

"There," the former lawman says, tapping his finger, "is where I reckon they'll head next."

How he knows this, Ted isn't sure. Mrs. Webster had asked him the previous night over dinner if he was in any danger of being killed when he'd told her that they were hot on the trail of Bonnie and Clyde.

"Well, there is always that possibility," he said to her. "No matter what."

"Oh, dear," she said.

She had prepared a pot roast and served with it whole boiled potatoes and green beans cooked in strips of bacon and some freshly baked rolls.

"Where are your children?" Ted asked, curious.

"Oh, they've gone to my mother's for the weekend — she lives in Fort Worth and I drove them there this morning."

"I see." Ted complimented her on the pot roast. For dessert they had apple pie and coffee. It reminded him of the old days when he'd walk his route and stop in Marco's Café and have pie and coffee, and of Bonnie, her cute smile.

After dinner, they sat in the living room with the radio on but turned way down and drank a glass of wine each and it was as though the whole while Mrs. Webster was waiting for someone, or something, to happen, and Ted had said, "You aren't expecting Mr. Webster to come home tonight, are you?" Feeling for the first time in his life guilty of a pleasure he hadn't partaken in — except for that very first night he'd stopped over there — and Mrs. Webster said, "No, Ted, I'm not."

They listened a little while longer to the music and finally Mrs. Webster said, "I believe this wine is going straight to my head," and fanned herself with her open hand. Ted didn't know if it was some sort of effort to change the mood or not, so instead he made an excuse that he had to get up early and that he'd better be going.

"Why it is only seven-thirty," Mrs. Webster

said. "Can't you possibly stay longer?"

He thought about it, then said no, he'd better get going, and she walked him to the door. He didn't know whether to try to kiss her good night or not. It felt awfully awkward. She touched his arm and said, "Thank you for sharing some of your evening with me, Ted. It was nice having a gentleman for company."

He kissed her cheek, promising himself once more that he would not see her again. She offered him the tiniest sigh when he kissed her, and he thought how easy it would be just to go on into the bedroom with her and stay the night. That was the problem with sin — it was just so damn easy.

"You be careful now, Ted, I'd hate to hear any bad news about you," she said just before he put his hat on. Her loneliness and his seemed to dog his heels all the way back to his apartment.

"If they hold true to form, and I believe they will," Frank Hamer is saying, "we'll have them in our sights before they know it."

"We going to ask them to give themselves up, or just start shooting?" Bob Alcorn asks.

"Would you give a mad dog a chance to bite you?" Frank says.

"I guess I wouldn't."

"Neither would I."

Ted remembers how good Mrs. Webster's apple pie was, the softness of her cheek when he kissed it, the way the night felt walking home alone and how it felt after, when he was alone in his own bed thinking about her being alone in her bed.

It was plenty odd, life was. He could still taste that pie.

22

The Eye of Love

Crickets infest their dreams. Twice Bonnie awakens and sees silvery light against one wall of plaster and lath. The light is moon that falls through an opposite window bereft of curtains. She's always been fearful of eyes watching her through windows.

"What you doing?" Clyde mumbles sleepily.

"Hanging a bedsheet over this window," she says.

There are two bent nails where a curtain rod once attached and from these she hangs the sheet.

Clyde sees her lithe body outlined against moonlight and linen, feels the pulse in his temple quicken.

"What's that sound?"

"Crickets," she says.

They bestir any further thought of rest. The night is warm, damp, sprinkled with humus. A breeze tries to lift but dies easily.

"Henry's daddy didn't seem very pleased to have us here."

"He's an unhappy drunk," Clyde says, sitting up, reaching for his package of cigarettes on the floor there by the bed.

"Still . . ."

"He won't give us any trouble. I've known his kind all my life. Big mouths and braggarts, tough when they're drunk, meek when they're sober."

"Oh, honey, I'm feeling like we can't go on this way much longer."

"Don't talk that way. You know how I hate that sort of talk."

But Bonnie broods. The night is so heavy, so dark and unyielding.

Clyde lights two cigarettes, extends one to her. She takes it, draws deeply into her lungs the dry smoke, picks a bit of tobacco from her tongue. There is nothing gentle about the way she feels.

"It gets so I hate night," she says, sitting on the side of the bed.

"Not me, honey. Night is the best time. Nobody can see you in the night, and if they can't see you, they can't catch you."

"I think that when I die I don't want it to be at night," Bonnie says.

Clyde slides out of bed, goes to the window, pulls the sheet aside, and looks out. Nothing. The yard, what there is of it, is weed-choked and unkempt and full of moonlight. A man could walk all the way across Louisiana in that much light. He doesn't like it.

"I think that when we die," he says, "we'll both be old and ready for it."

Of course he is trying to lift her spirits, as always when she gets like this. He knows she misses her kin and will begin soon to beg him to take her back to see her mama. He knows that every time they return to Dallas there is a greater chance the laws will catch them.

But he misses his kin too. He thinks of old Buck lying in a lonely grave covered with this very same moonlight. In his head he holds a conversation with his late brother.

How you doing, old son? What's it like to be dead? Is it like stepping off a ledge into darkness?

But Buck, he don't answer.

Bonnie wishes they had a radio at least.

She hears Henry's daddy off in another room talking. Then something loud crashes, like a chair knocked over or a pan fallen, then all is silence again. Clyde continues to look out the window.

He sees the old man stumbling across the yard to the outhouse. Sees him fall to his knees, then try and rise again, but finally giving up and just kneeling that way. There is something pitiful about such human decline. Clyde feels the sudden urge to go out and shoot the old man, thinking it would be a gesture of kindness. But hell, it's Henry's daddy and after all, you don't just shoot the kin of people you know because they are pitiful or unwise.

"I'm feeling all troubled, Clyde."

Bonnie is there on the bed, her legs crossed, smoking the cigarette, the red glow of it illuminating her face every time she inhales.

"What do you want me to do, honey?"

"Take away my blues, Clyde."

"I don't know how to take away your blues, sugar."

"At least try, okay?"

He comes away from the window and kneels at her feet.

"No, baby, not like that," she says. "I don't mean like that . . ."

"Then like what?"

"Oh, I don't know . . ."

Ted Hinton and Bob Alcorn are driving in one car. Ahead of them in another car is

Frank Hamer and Manny Gault.

"Smell that," Bob says.

They have the windows rolled down and the swampy night air is dank and thick.

"Smells like a place you wouldn't want to go walking alone without a gun," Bob says.

Bob has a fascination with dangerous creatures, like poisonous snakes, and since they've crossed the line into Louisiana — alligators, too.

"I don't think you could even kill one of them big gators with a pistol much under a forty-five," Bob said not long into the swamp country.

But Ted isn't thinking about alligators or poisonous snakes or walks into the swamp. He is thinking about Mrs. Webster this night. He wonders if her husband has returned from his latest business trip and if she fixed him a nice dinner while he played with the children. He wonders if later they sat in the living room and listened to the radio and had a glass of wine together. He wonders if by now they've climbed the stairs up to the bedroom together and gotten into bed and are holding each other.

It'd be nice, he thinks, being in a clean soft bed right now instead of driving through this strange swampy country he has no familiarity with. It would be nice to have somebody you love there in bed with you — to sleep in loving peace together. It'd be nice to make love and then close your eyes to a blissful sleep . . .

"Why what are they stopping for?" Bob says, slowing the automobile. Up ahead, Frank has pulled over to the side of the road, his taillights bright as two cherries. Seems old Frank's caught a nail or something sharp, for his front tire has gone flat.

Bob pulls over and he and Ted get out and walk up to where Frank is standing beside the lopsided coupe.

"We seem to be having the most extraordinary bad luck of catching up to those two . . ." Frank is saying to Manny. "But we'll catch 'em."

"I don't know about you boys," says Bob, "but that beer I drank in that last café we stopped at is begging me to leave it right here in the great state of Louisiana . . ." and steps out of the glare of the headlights to relieve himself.

"Careful there, Bob," Manny says. "Some gator will chomp your cigar off."

They laugh a little, then patch the tire, taking a good hour off their time.

A rooster crows down the morning from

atop a fence post that leans under the weight of time. Whatever fence the post used to support has long since disappeared into the disrepair of weeds.

Bonnie emerges from the house with red-rimmed eyes from crying half the night.

There on the little porch sits Henry shoeless.

"I'm an early riser," he explains, as though Bonnie has asked him about his appearance.

The sun is yet low and splintered through the trunks of trees off to the east, and whatever wind this land once held, it holds no more.

"It's as still as a dead man, ain't it," Henry says. "Always this way this time of year unless you get a hurricane coming up from the Gulf. Then it blows like hell. Blow the damn feathers off a chicken. It's always one way or the other, never nothing in between, like a gentle breeze."

Bonnie has never known Henry to talk this much. His uncommon effusiveness just adds to her odd feeling. She does not encourage him further by trying to hold a conversation.

Clyde emerges from the house letting the screen door slap shut like a pistol shot, small caliber.

"Morning," he says.

"Good morning, Clyde," Henry says. "Still as a dead man, ain't it?"

Clyde is hatless and runs his fingers through his mussed hair.

"I heard a rooster crow," Clyde says.

"I know it," says Henry. "Damn thing is, I never known my daddy to own a rooster or a chicken or nothing else either."

It seems a small mystery that none of them cares to solve.

Bonnie says, "I'd like to go for a walk, Clyde."

"Go on then, old Henry won't mind, will you, Henry?"

Henry shakes his head.

"No, I mean the two of us, honey," she says.

They don't walk very far before Clyde says, "The dew's getting my pant legs wet, honey."

"Oh, never mind that."

They walk a hedgerow, past an old harrow somebody's long since abandoned, its teeth rusty, the weeds grown up around it. Their stroll scares up a hare — a gray bony creature with ragged ears that zigs and zags till it reaches the edge of a wood where it pauses briefly to look back, then disappears under a rotting log.

"How far you reckon we are going to need to walk?" Clyde says, picking cockleburs off the cuff of his trousers.

"Oh, I don't know. I'd like to just keep walking all the way to Egypt," Bonnie says, her voice full of sorrow.

"Egypt, huh?"

"I just don't know what we're going to do anymore, honey . . ."

He puts his arm around her waist. He never ceases to be amazed at what a tiny waist she has.

"Don't worry, sugar. Old Clyde's never let you down yet. I'll figure us a way out of all this."

They stop and look back at the shotgun house. How small it seems. How incomplete in the grand scheme of dreams.

"No you won't," Bonnie says to Clyde. "You won't figure a way out of this for us . . ."

He would like to repudiate her claim, to disavow her of any such notion.

But her eyes tell a story he has no ending for.

We'll just keep going on . . .
Going on until we're put out like Lottie's eye.

A silly thing his daddy used to say . . .

251

23

Love's Last Journey

What's all the commotion, Mama? Why's everybody in the house?

They've all come to see you, sweet child of mine.

See me?

Yes, yes.

But if they've come to see me, why then are they all gathered in the parlor?

Because that is where you lie, sweet child. There, where once you sang and danced in your pretty little dress and pretty little shoes — when you were ten and I was just twenty.

She is wearing a peach dress and the pillow beneath her head is white satin.

Somber faces slowly pass by, their muted lips whispering. Her sister Billie, often mistaken for Bonnie herself, has eyes full of tears. Her mama's wail is like a distant siren.

The dream does startle her awake.

Clyde looks stricken.

"You were having a nightmare," says he. "You were screaming in your sleep. It scared the hell out of me."

"Oh, God, honey, it was so real."

"What was?"

"The dream of my funeral."

"Oh, Christ, don't talk of such things."

But the dream realized seems no less real. It clings to her, claws at the very essence of that part of her she has learned to think of as *soul*.

"Do you think Jesus will forgive us our sins?" she asks Clyde.

"I don't know much about Jesus," he says. "What he will or won't forgive. I never got that far into all that stuff."

"Me either, baby, that's what scares me — I don't know that much about God."

"My folks was always believing," Clyde recounts. "Even when we was living under that damn bridge. I don't know how they could believe in any God who'd let us live worse than niggers if He was as good-hearted as they say."

"I can't believe He'd let them just kill us." Bonnie bites her lower lip, fretful, afraid for once of the inevitable weight time carries with it. Afraid that no matter the number of their days, such days will never be enough, and she will never be brave enough to face actual death.

"I just hope when they do kill us," says she, "that it is quick and painless. Do you think it will be, Clyde?"

"I've been shot and I can tell you there ain't nothing painless about it. But of course I never been shot fatally, so I can't say."

"When the time comes, I want to have time to pray," Bonnie says. "I want to be able to beg Jesus to take me in."

"Maybe you could ask Him to take us both in while you're at it."

"Oh, Clyde, don't make light of such things . . ."

Her fear strangely enough stirs his desire for her.

He has often wondered whether fear is the food that feeds the beast of a man's lust — whether it fed the lust of Chicago Willy when he took that boy back in the pen, then later slit his throat.

"I need you to do something for me," Clyde says.

"What, honey?"

"Get on the bed."

She does, wordlessly, and he pushes up her skirt. It seems an odd time for such doings, but in her hunger for something of life to cling to, she clings to Clyde while he makes hasty work of his unbidden desire, then rolls away, breathing hard, feeling hollow inside.

"It's going to be okay," he says. "Everything is going to be okay."

And while the lovers couple, the half-sober daddy of Henry Methvin is in Shreveport with a tall man sitting under a cowboy hat. Their conspiracy is hatched at the counter of a drugstore where sundaes and lemon phosphates are sold to quench parched throats. They do conspire to bring to an end the reign of terror that has plagued at least four states for the last two years, that has left men dead and their widows grieving and empty cash registers everywhere.

"All I want is a pardon for my boy," the man with the same turtle eyes as his son says.

"That can be arranged, I'm sure. I know the governor of Texas pretty well," says Frank Hamer.

They close the deal, seal the bargain, tie the Gordian knot.

"Your boy," Frank Hamer says, "you need to make sure he is not with them at the appointed hour."

"I'll make sure, even if I have to knock a knot on his head."

Frank Hamer lays four bits on the counter to pay for their soft drinks.

Hardly thirty pieces of silver this . . .

Upon his exit from the drugstore, the man with turtle eyes slips down an alley, up a back stairs, and pays a man for a jar of shine, which he drinks on the way home satisfied he has done the right thing. Henry may not have amounted to much, he reasons, but he don't deserve to get shot down like a dog.

Lovers know little more than what lovers know. And in their need to shake the heavy mood, Clyde and Bonnie, and their friend Henry, drive into Arcadia to buy some burgers. For red beans and dry-as-sand cornbread so much of the time have advanced their state of depression, their feeling of isolation.

They drive along the country road, their gloom lifting just a bit at the thought of "getting out" even if for a little while.

"Can we go to the picture show?" Bonnie asks.

"There ain't one in Arcadia," Henry says, "but there is one in Shreveport."

Clyde considers turning around and heading to Shreveport, but they are too far along and tells Bonnie, "Tomorrow we go to Shreveport to the movies."

But instantly she expresses her concern about the laws.

"We'll go in the evening," Clyde says. "Go to the late feature."

"I remember seeing they were playing *The Thin Man* when we drove through there the other night," Bonnie says.

"The Rialto," Henry says. "That's the name of the movie house."

"Can we go see it?"

"Sure," Clyde says, "though I don't care that much for Ronald Coleman."

"What about you, Henry? Do you like Ronald Coleman?" Bonnie asks.

"I never met the guy. What's he like?"

Bonnie and Clyde laugh. Henry is such a hick.

Henry instructs Clyde to a café there in Arcadia — The Hometown. Clyde pulls to the curb, gives Henry a few dollars to go in and get them all some burgers.

"No onion on mine," Bonnie says.

"Henry," they say in unison as they watch him saunter into the café.

"After the next job, we'll cut him loose," Clyde says.

"He's nice enough but a little dense," says Bonnie.

"Yeah, that thing with the two motorcycle cops," replies Clyde. "Jesus, what a fuck up."

Bonnie squeezes Clyde's hand, says, "I know it, honey. He might just as well put us in the chair and pull the switch."

"You understand, don't you, sugar. You understand everything there is about this game."

"Nobody understands it like we do, Clyde. Fate dealt us the same hand."

Henry is inside taking his time. Clyde and Bonnie can see him through the plate-glass window, sitting at the counter, talking to the waitress, who is plump and wears a little paper waitress hat.

"The hell's he doing?" Clyde says nervously.

Bonnie shakes her head. These Louisiana fellows aren't real swift.

Then the next any of them knows, a police car pulls up to the curb and two officers get out wearing dark uniforms with white piping down their pant legs and heavy pistols hanging from their hips. They are lean and take their time, talking, one of them nods his head.

Without saying a word, Clyde starts the V-8 and drives away.

"What about Henry?" Bonnie says.

"We'll pick him up later."

Bonnie looks back and through the rear window sees the two policemen enter the café. She can't remember if Henry is armed. And later, when Clyde comes 'round again, cruises down the same street and sees the patrol car is no longer parked in front of the café, they see too the stool at the counter where Henry sat chatting with the fat waitress now empty.

Clyde drives up and down the few streets but they are void of one Henry Methvin.

There are guesses of course as to his fate. Clyde's guess is that he went out the back door and made his way home. Bonnie isn't so sure when they don't come across Henry along the road on the way back to his daddy's place.

And no sign of Henry in the little shotgun shack, and no sign of his daddy either, puts Bonnie and Clyde on high alert.

"Something's wrong," Clyde says.

"I feel it too."

They pack hastily.

"We need to scat."

"Yes, we must."

"Where to, baby?"

Clyde half smiles.

"Make a run for the border?"

"Why not?"

"We'll ride the coast of the Gulf all the way to Mexico."

Bonnie is both happy and sad at once. She will miss her mama, but Mexico is the current symbol of a new life — a fresh start.

She is so happy she kisses Clyde. He returns the kiss.

The weight of his automatic rifle strains Ted Hinton's arm muscles. His thoughts are quick and nervous. He and the others stand in ambuscade among the hardwoods along what Mr. Methvin calls the "old Sailes Road." The mosquitoes prove a nuisance.

It's just a common dirt road — an inglorious place to die.

In the grand scheme of things, only the executioner can choose the time and place of death. *It's my job,* Ted keeps repeating to himself.

His companions stand ready.

They have parked Mr. Methvin's old truck across the road. Made it to look like it is broken down, by knocking the front wheel off.

Otherwise, it is just another pleasant morning.

Bonnie traces their progress on a road

map spread out across her knees. She has chosen for their journey her favorite red dress. And Clyde is looking very debonair in the dark glasses he wears to shade his eyes. His tan fedora rides at a jaunty angle, raked low over his brow.

"I want to go swimming in the Gulf of Mexico," Bonnie says, seeing the large blue water on the map.

"Be my guest," Clyde says. "You know how I feel about swimming."

"Oh, pooh," she says teasingly. "Won't you go in with me?"

"No, I won't."

She starts to sing a torch song she has come to love — "Love Me or Leave Me."

Clyde thinks she has a pretty good voice.

"You should have become a singer," he says.

The road rises ahead of them, and there at its apex, Clyde sees Henry's daddy's old truck cockeyed off the side of the road. He eases off the gas pedal, shifts the car into a lower gear to make the grade.

Bonnie has her eyes closed, singing about love.

Bob Alcorn says, "That's them, boys."

"Wait till I give the word," Frank Hamer instructs.

Ted brings up his rifle, so do the others.

Bonnie hardly notices Clyde's slowing of the V-8, so engrossed is she in the melancholy of the song's words.

Clyde's eyes scan the area right around the abandoned truck.

"What the hell," he says.

This is when Bonnie opens her eyes, at the sound of mild alarm in Clyde's voice.

"What's wrong, honey."

"I don't guess anything . . ."

She can hardly speak. Her words stuck there in her heart as Clyde, her eternal love, is tossed to and fro, as bloody marks do appear like bursts of red paint upon him, face and hands and everywhere.

She wants to say, *Do not leave me!*

For a moment, his dark glasses knocked from his eyes, he does turn to stare at her.

I won't leave you . . .the eyes seem to say.

She barely feels the dying.

Even while flung about.

And suddenly Clyde is slumping over the wheel, then being knocked back again before her blurry vision, even as they steal the breath from her, this invisible death.

It all comes down to this . . .This world of the dimming light and growing darkness, of shattered bone and flesh she is becoming.

And poor Clyde, naught but a bloody rag doll.

. . . poor, poor Clyde,

and reaches for him but cannot lift even her frail broken arm.

Cannot reach her love and touch him one last time, his hat there on the floor at her feet, bloodstained, upturned. The showering glass cuts her pretty face.

Oh, God, Clyde . . .

Then feels at last herself drawn down into a safer darker place where a pinprick of light does shine way off in the distance. And she wonders if maybe, just maybe, the light she sees is the sun shining on the Gulf of Mexico.

POSTSCRIPT

Ray Hamilton was executed in the electric chair at Huntsville Prison thirteen months after the death of Bonnie and Clyde.

W. D. Jones wrote of his adventures with Bonnie and Clyde in an article in *Playboy* magazine in 1968. He was later murdered in Houston, Texas, by an unknown assailant.

Henry Methvin served ten years in an Oklahoma prison for his crimes and misdeeds and was later killed in a train accident.

Emma Parker and Cummie Barrow, the mothers of Bonnie and Clyde, were each sentenced to short jail terms for helping their children evade the law. Other members of the Barrow family served various sentences as well.

Blanche Barrow, Buck Barrow's widow, was sentenced to fifteen years in prison for her activities with Bonnie and Clyde. Upon her release, she disappeared from public view.

Ralph Fults began speaking publicly against crime upon his release from Huntsville Prison. He died an old man in 1993.

Frank Hamer died from the effects of a stroke in 1955.

Ted Hinton quit the police force and bought a motel. He wrote a book about Bonnie and Clyde — *Ambush*. He passed away in 1977.

Bonnie and Clyde are both buried in Dallas, but not together, as had been Bonnie's wish. Each had suffered more than fifty bullet wounds in the ambush. Bonnie died still wearing the simple gold wedding ring Roy Thornton put on her finger when he married her.

Bonnie was twenty-three years old at the time of her death. Clyde was just twenty-four.

About the Author

BILL BROOKS is the author of nine novels, including *The Badmen, Buscadero, Return to No Man's Land,* and the western classic *The Stone Garden: The Epic Life of Billy the Kid.* A professor at Asheville Buncombe Community College, Bill Brooks lives with his wife in the Blue Ridge Mountains of North Carolina.

The employees of Thorndike Press hope you have enjoyed this Large Print book. All our Thorndike and Wheeler Large Print titles are designed for easy reading, and all our books are made to last. Other Thorndike Press Large Print books are available at your library, through selected bookstores, or directly from us.

For information about titles, please call:

(800) 223-1244

or visit our Web site at:

www.gale.com/thorndike
www.gale.com/wheeler

To share your comments, please write:

Publisher
Thorndike Press
295 Kennedy Memorial Drive
Waterville, ME   04901